# LARRABEE'S LUCK

Other books by Jane McBride Choate:

*All That I Ask*
*Cheyenne's Rainbow Warrior*
*Convincing David*
*Desert Paintbox*
*Heartsong Lullaby*
*A Match Made In Heaven*
*Mile-High Love*
*Never Too Late for Christmas*
*Sheriff's Choice*
*Star Crossed*
*Think of Me*
*Wolf's Eye*

# LARRABEE'S LUCK

•

Jane McBride Choate

*AVALON BOOKS*
NEW YORK

Published by Avalon Books,
an imprint of Thomas Bouregy & Co., Inc.
160 Madison Avenue, New York, NY 10016

Library of Congress Cataloging-in-Publication Data

Choate, Jane McBride.
Larrabee's luck / Jane McBride Choate.
p. cm.
ISBN 978-0-8034-7717-9 (acid-free paper) 1. Women ranchers—Fiction. 2. Horse trainers—Fiction. 3. Colorado—History—19th century—Fiction. I. Title.
PS3553.H575L37 2011
813'.54—dc22

2010031079

PRINTED IN THE UNITED STATES OF AMERICA
ON ACID-FREE PAPER
BY HADDON CRAFTSMEN, BLOOMSBURG, PENNSYLVANIA

*To my Uncle Vearl and Aunt Betty and their love story,*
*which has lasted over sixty-five years*

# *Prologue*

*The Silver Lady Mine, ten miles north of Denver, 1876*

"We're all gonna die."

The words so closely echoed Cade's own thoughts that his voice was sharper than he intended. "We're not gonna die. Not today anyway."

He only prayed he could make good on his words. Twelve men were counting on him. Twelve men who had wives and children counting on them. Twelve men who would surely die unless he did something.

The men's fear was palpable. So was his own. He tasted it, smelled it, breathed it. Funny, he'd never realized that fear had a smell. A sickly sweet smell, like apple cider gone bad. It clung to him, to each of the men clustered together.

His mouth thinned into a grim line. *Okay, Larrabee. Find a way out of this and do it quick.*

He looked at the pile of rocks blocking the exit to the silver mine and thought of the men he'd left on the outside when he'd entered this death trap. They'd be working frantically to clear the entrance. Even now, they were probably clearing away the rubble.

The air was stale, the walls damp. The flickering light from oil lamps cast eerie shadows.

The miners needed to do something, anything, to hold on to the hope that they'd be rescued. The longer they remained in the mine, the greater their chances of running out of air. Any physical exertion would use up the rapidly shrinking air supply even more quickly. Cade measured that danger against the need for hope.

He chose hope.

"C'mon," he ordered the men huddled against the dank walls. "We're getting out of here."

"How're we gonna do that?" the self-appointed leader of the men challenged.

Cade met his hard gaze with one of his own. "One rock at a time."

Painstakingly, Cade and the others hauled away the rocks. He discovered that if he took measured, shallow breaths, it helped minimize the effects of the rapidly evaporating air. Despite his efforts, though, sweat streamed down his face and neck, his lungs working like a blacksmith's bellows.

He tore off his shirt, then ripped away a sleeve to tie around his forehead to sop up the sweat. His breathing grew heavier, his chest tighter, until he struggled for every gulp of air. Breath rushed in and out of his lungs with a harsh, rhythmic gasp. His arms and shoulders screamed with pain as he pushed himself to keep hauling away rocks.

Several of the men had given up and slumped against the walls, eyes closed, jaws slack, chests heaving.

After what felt like hours, Cade held up a hand. "Listen."

The clink of metal against stone sounded above the men's labored breathing.

"We're here," one of the men shouted. "In here." The others added their voices to the cry.

A few minutes later, an opening appeared. Air filtered in, tasting sweeter than the most expensive wine.

One by one, the miners climbed through the hole. Cade waited until everyone else was out before he made his own escape.

"You did it." The leader clapped Cade on the back.

"*We* did it." Cade sucked in gulps of air. Ignoring the cheers of the men, he made his way to the foreman of the mine.

Cade closed his fist around the man's shirt and hauled him up to his toes. "This mine should have been shut down months ago. You knew about the rotting timbers, but you chose to ignore it. You sent good men in there to die."

"I didn't know the timbers were going to collapse. No one could have known. I stand by my decision to keep it open." The foreman jerked away from Cade's grip. "Closing it down would have cost General Wingate thousands of dollars."

"And how many lives?" Cade's voice turned soft. The men who knew him backed up a few paces. "No men go back inside until the timbers are replaced and everything is shored up. Do I make myself clear?"

"You got no call talking to me that way. I take my orders from the general and nobody else."

"Wrong. You take your orders from me. I'm not going anywhere until this mine is safe." Cade fixed the other man with a hard look. "You'll want to make certain because you're going to be the first one back inside."

## *Chapter One*

*Denver*

Folding beefy arms across a barrel chest, General Victor Wingate, retired, glared at Cade Larrabee. "You cost me a passel of money at the Silver Lady. Spending good money to replace timbers."

Florid color swept up his neck to settle on already flushed cheeks. He leaned forward and stabbed a thick finger in Cade's direction. "There'll be no return on that investment."

No mention of the lives that were almost lost. Cade hadn't expected anything different. Something inside him was starting to give. He'd known it for months now. He felt a dissatisfaction that he'd never before experienced and a longing for something he couldn't name. "So hire someone else." The indifference in his voice was calculated to raise the general's ire.

"You know you're the best." The muttered words held no warmth and only a grudging admiration. With an effort, the general stood. Age and hard living had caused his once proud bearing to be slightly stooped. "I want you to find a woman for me."

Cade leaned easily against the massive desk in the oak-paneled library and grinned. "Can't you find one on your own?"

"Not just any woman. A particular one."

"Business?"

"It's personal."

"Why me?"

The older man braced himself on his desk. "If I could do it myself, I would. But I can't, and there's no one else I trust enough."

The grin fell from Cade's face.

All his life, he had known when trouble was on the way. This peculiar sense had saved his life on more than one occasion. Which was why the meeting today with his boss had left him feeling edgy. Anxious. Like a wolf that smells smoke in the wind, sensing peril, ready to run, but uncertain in which direction safety lies.

Cade had served as the general's aide-de-camp during the war. When the general had resigned, Cade had resigned his commission as well, doing whatever was needed for Wingate's vast holdings in mining, ranching, and banking.

Never one to want to stay in one place for any length of time, Cade liked what he did. He understood himself well enough to know that he needed variety and challenge.

He was accustomed to dealing with problems, but he had never before been asked to handle matters in the general's personal life. He wasn't even sure the old man *had* a personal life, outside of his sister.

Wingate had little use for anyone or anything that did not help build his already staggering wealth.

"What's so special about it?" Cade asked. "Why can't one of your regular people handle it?"

"It's personal," Wingate repeated testily. He was not a man accustomed to explaining himself.

"What else?"

"That's it," the general said, voice casual as a shrug.

Cade raised an eyebrow. Wingate was lying. Cade knew it. What's more, Wingate knew Cade knew.

Wingate shifted his gaze away from Cade and coughed. "Well, what are you waiting for?"

"The truth."

The older man's face twisted in displeasure. "I want her found. That's the only truth you need to know."

Cade waited. He'd learned a long time ago that patience achieved more than arguing ever did.

Wingate gave a disgruntled *harrumph.* "You're a stubborn cuss, you know that?"

Cade remained silent. It was a trick he'd picked up in the army. It put him in good stead then. And now.

The general sighed. "The woman I'm looking for is my niece."

"Your niece?"

"That's right. Trudy's child."

Cade tried to make sense of that. As far as he knew, the general's sister had never been married, never had any children. "You might as well tell me the rest of it."

"That's it." Wingate grunted when Cade made no comment. "Twenty-eight years ago, Trudy made a fool of herself over a man, a no-account drifter. He left her.

Just like I told her he would. She had the child. We agreed it was best to put it up for adoption."

Cade understood the stigma of a woman having a child out of wedlock, especially a woman of Trudy Wingate's social station. Denver society would never have accepted her or the child. Both would have been ostracized, shunned by those who called themselves friends.

"Trudy wanted to keep the child, said she didn't care what people thought. I reminded her she had a responsibility to the family not to drag the Wingate name through the mud."

A soft hiss escaped Cade's lips. He bit his lower lip and tasted blood. Whatever her mistakes, no one deserved that kind of pressure heaped upon her, especially a young girl scarcely out of the schoolroom.

"So you forced her to give up her child."

"Trudy listens to me."

Four words, but they said much. Victor Wingate, former general in the Union army, demanded total obedience from those who served under him—his troops, his employees, his sister.

When it came to conflict, General Victor Wingate had never settled for anything less than total victory. Not in battle. Not in business. Not in his personal life.

"We gave the child to a missionary couple who were passing through. They promised to place her with a good family."

The careless tone said he hadn't cared what kind of family the child was placed with.

Something in the general's eyes, a look that said there was more to it than what he'd let on, caused Cade's gut to clench. He'd learned to trust that feeling. "Not interested.

Give it to Murdock," he said, naming one of Wingate's top men.

"You have an older brother, don't you?" Wingate asked in a musing tone. "Noah. Served the Union under McClellan."

"So?" The abrupt change of subject increased Cade's wariness.

"A certain letter's come into my possession, a letter concerning your brother. Perhaps you'd like to read it."

Cade took the much-folded letter and scanned it. His lips tightened as he read it through once more. A furrow worked its way between his brows. The words condemned Noah as a coward who had deserted in the face of enemy fire.

"It's nothing but a pack of lies."

"You sure about that?" The general struck a pose, gnarled fingers stroking his jaw. He held Cade's gaze, his eyes hard with shrewdness and cunning intelligence.

"Of course . . ." Cade paused.

Noah had never talked much about that time. Cade had always attributed Noah's reluctance to a natural desire to avoid any reminder of the War Between the States, a war that had cost him his legs. He never even displayed the medal of bravery he'd received, preferring to keep it hidden away.

"You don't believe me. Maybe you'll believe these." Wingate thrust a sheaf of papers into Cade's hands.

Inspecting them, he saw they supported the letter. "Where do I start?"

The satisfied smirk on Wingate's lips rasped against Cade's already frayed nerves.

"Glad you see it my way."

Cade turned, paused. "Would you have allowed Trudy to keep the child had it been a boy?"

It hadn't taken long.

"I've found her," Cade stated without preliminaries. Seated once more in the general's library, he kept his face carefully blank. From past experience he knew little escaped the older man's notice.

"It didn't take you long."

"No," Cade agreed. "It didn't."

"Where?"

"Just south of the Springs," he said.

"What's her name? What's she doing?"

"Johanna Kellerman. She runs a few hundred head of cattle and trains horses on the side."

Wingate placed his fingers together steeple-fashion. "Anything else?"

Cade thought of what he'd learned about Johanna Kellerman. "She's well liked and respected. Her outfit is small but growing." He studied Wingate before asking the question that had been on his mind since the older man had blackmailed him into taking the job. "When are you going to tell Trudy?"

The general frowned. "I hired you to do a job, not ask questions."

Neat evasion. Counter with an attack. Cade shouldn't have been surprised. The general had used the tactic enough while in the military.

Wingate lowered his gaze. A twitch of his jaw muscles exposed his displeasure. And something more.

"Well, what are you waiting for?"

"What?" Still immersed in his own thoughts, Cade stared blankly at him.

"Get close to her, find out what she's like, what puts a spur under her saddle."

"I told you. She has a small spread, trying to get a start in the horse-training business. She has a good name in the area."

Wingate snapped his fingers. "That's nothing. I want to know who she is. If she needs money. What she's willing to do to get it."

"Why?"

"Because that's why I'm paying you." A large vein in the general's neck bulged, betraying his annoyance.

"Correction—you blackmailed me into finding her. Nothing less, nothing more."

"You like Trudy, don't you?"

The question took Cade by surprise. He had a soft spot for the general's sister. Quiet, fragile-looking Trudy Wingate was the opposite of her brother in every respect. He'd talked with her casually over the years, liking her quick wit and gentle manner. Stricken with arthritis early in life, Trudy stayed close to home.

"If it weren't for Trudy's health," Wingate said, rubbing his cheek reflectively, "I wouldn't be so concerned. But she's delicate. Especially now. I don't want to see her hurt."

"Why now? Why do you want to find her daughter after all these years?"

"I don't." The general look irritated. "It's Trudy. She's got some fool notion she wants to see her child. I tried to tell her she doesn't know what kind of trouble she's opening up, but she can be mighty stubborn when she wants."

"It might be good for her to see her daughter. Didn't you say Trudy's been depressed lately? I think—"

"You're not paid to think. You're paid to get results. I don't want Trudy involved. I told her I'd take care of it, and that's what I intend to do."

Cade stared at the man who had been first his commanding officer and then his boss for over a dozen years, his gaze unwavering.

"You wanted to say something?" Wingate asked.

"Yeah." With a casualness that belied his inner tension, Cade poured himself a drink from the crystal decanter sitting on the desk. "If I go back, it will be on my own terms. I'll find out what you want, but I do it my way."

Wingate gave him a measured look.

Cade returned it with one of his own. Cold gray eyes clashed with brown.

The general was the first to look away.

*The Double J Ranch, just south of Colorado Springs*

Johanna Kellerman stabbed her fingers through her hair. Balancing accounts would never come first on her list of things to do, but the figures had come out right.

For once.

That was the good news. The bad news was that the balance was precariously low. Another good year, maybe two, and she'd be free of debt.

Straightening her shoulders, she focused on the positive. The Double J was showing a profit and establishing a small but growing reputation among horsemen. If she did a good job, she could count on a recommendation from Mr. Patterson. One of the biggest ranchers in the area, Charlie Patterson carried a lot of influence. A word from him could make her reputation—or break it.

In addition, she had another job, a referral from a satisfied client. The problem was having enough men to keep the operation going.

She pushed her chair back from her makeshift desk of a slab of wood stretched across two sawhorses. Coffee stains, scratches, and scars covered its surface. It wasn't much to look at, but it was practical.

Bill Riedman had up and quit today. He'd given no explanation, just said he had to be moving on. She shook her head, sending her already-tousled curls into further abandon.

"Just what we need," she muttered to herself. "One less man when we're already short."

"Hey, Boss, got a minute?"

She looked up at George Gardner, her foreman. George was a bear of a man who adored his young wife. Would she ever find a man who loved her as completely as George loved his Sarah?

Loneliness swamped her as she thought of the love Sarah and George shared for each other. Did they realize how truly blessed they were? With the death of her father, Johanna had no one. Even though Johanna recognized the foolishness of it, her heart ached for something she had never known.

George had thinning hair, the beginnings of a paunch,

and a perpetual grin. He'd still been in his teens when he'd come to work for her father nearly twenty years ago. Today, the grin was conspicuously absent.

"Sure. What's on your mind?"

"The men . . ." He cleared his throat. "We're all sort of wondering if you're gonna hire on another man."

Johanna sighed. She knew the men were spread thin as it was. "I know. Tell them I'm working on it, okay?"

"Okay." He paused, shuffling from one foot to the other, a sure sign he was unhappy with what he had to tell her.

"Is there something else?"

"It's Sarah," George said, naming his wife and the light of his life. "She's hinting for me to take a job with one of the big outfits. She don't want to leave you. Ain't neither of us want that. It's just with the baby coming . . ."

Johanna resisted the urge to indulge in a good cry. George Gardner was not only her foreman; he was her best friend. If he quit, she'd be lost in more ways than one. His wife, Sarah, was housekeeper, ranch cook, and friend.

"It's not that I don't like working here." He lifted his hands, a silent gesture of appeal. "Sarah feels real bad about this, just 'bout as bad as I do, but she says we gotta think about the baby."

"I know," Johanna said, struggling to keep the dismay from her voice. "I don't blame you for wanting to work for a bigger outfit. I can't match them in wages." *And probably never will be able to,* she added to herself.

George had married late in life to a woman half his age. Proving the town gossips wrong, George and Sarah appeared blissfully happy, especially since they'd learned Sarah was with child.

"If it was just me, I'd stick with you. For the first time in a long time, I feel good about what I'm doing. Your pa was a good man, but . . ."

Johanna nodded. After the death of her mother, her father had let the ranch go. His heart hadn't been in it anymore. The Double J, named for her mother, Jenny, and herself, had once been a showplace. The ramshackle buildings bore a mute testament to his neglect.

As always, the memory of her father caused a spasm of pain to move through her. At least one good thing had come from his death—her parents were now together again.

She shook off her melancholia and renewed her determination to make the Double J shine once more. In what few spare moments she could eke out, she was enlarging the barn in order to board and train more horses.

"You're doing a fine job, and I know you'll turn the place around, but I've got to look out for Sarah and the baby."

"I know," she said ruefully.

"I'll stick around for as long as I can. I just thought I ought to tell you for when . . ." He patted her awkwardly on the shoulder. "Just thought I ought to tell you."

"I appreciate it," she said around the lump in her throat. She waited until he let himself out before she let her shoulders droop into a defeated slump.

She didn't blame George. He had a wife to think of, a baby on the way. If he could do better with a bigger outfit, she couldn't—wouldn't—stand in his way.

*Leave tomorrow's trouble for tomorrow,* Jenny Kellerman had said often enough.

That was just what Johanna intended to do. She didn't need to go borrowing tomorrow's troubles. Right now, she had enough of today's.

Impatient with her ruminations, she pushed her chair back and stood. Her shoulders ached from the long hours hunched over account books. She smiled, acknowledging that she didn't notice any discomfort when she was shoveling manure or working with even the most cranky horse.

She wasn't cut out for the ciphering end of running a ranch, but she was learning.

Putting her desk in the barn had been a deliberate choice. She preferred working near the animals rather than in the house. She liked the sounds they made, the sight of them, the smells.

"Hey, Boss."

She turned to see Rudy, a ranch hand, walking her way, a tall, brown-haired man at his side. The stranger carried himself easily, his whipcord-lean body radiating the kind of confidence that said he was comfortable with who—and what—he was.

His dark brown eyes had an alertness that stopped just short of being overly intent. It was only when he moved nearer that she saw something in his expression, a shadow of pain that sparked something within her. A jagged scar started in the center of his forehead before veering into the hairline at his left temple.

"I think we might have a replacement for Bill," Rudy said.

"Cade Larrabee, ma'am." The man stuck out his hand.

She took it, liking the feel of his handshake. It was firm without being hard, gripping hers with a quiet strength that said he had no need to impress anyone. Her fingers encountered ridged calluses. She liked that.

"Johanna Kellerman."

She took her time studying him. He had the lean, tough muscles of a man accustomed to hard work. Resisting the urge to fidget under his assessing look, she waited while he completed his own inspection.

"Cade here's looking for work," Rudy put in when the silence between them stretched.

"What kind of work do you do?" she asked.

"A little bit of everything." Brown eyes, the color of rich, freshly turned earth, squinted in the sun's glare. "But given my choice, I prefer working with horses."

She shaded her own eyes and stared up at him. Since he must have topped six feet by several inches, it was a long way. "You know your way around horses?"

"You could say that." A faint smile chased across his lips.

"It's what you say that matters."

"Yeah." His smile deepened, a slow, chipped-tooth grin that did funny things to her insides. "I know my way around horses."

It was too much to hope for, but she asked it anyway. "You ever do any training?"

He rocked back on the heels of his boots, thumbs hooked in the pockets of his much-worn trousers. "Matter of fact, I've done a bit. It's been a while, though."

She couldn't believe her luck. "I'll show you what we're doing." She headed to the corral. When he didn't follow, she called over her shoulder, "Coming?"

"Yeah."

"She's a beauty, isn't she?" Johanna asked, pointing to where George was trying to bridle a two-year-old. A training saddle lay at his side. The fractious horse reared back. "Her name's Willow. She's a bit high-strung."

Cade nodded shortly. "Mind if I give it a try?" He reached inside his saddlebags and pulled out a black cloth, then climbed over the fence and walked to the center of the corral.

After getting a nod from Johanna, George handed the bridle to Cade.

Johanna watched as Cade gentled Willow with a word and a pat to her neck. No whips or quirts were used at the Double J. Any man who used a whip on an animal was fired on the spot.

"It's all right, girl," Cade said as he eased a hood over her head.

Johanna started in his direction, but George stayed her with a hand to her shoulder. "Let him show us what he can do."

Willow showed her displeasure by bucking. "None of that," Cade murmured and proceeded to lead her around the corral. "You're just showing off, aren't you?"

His pace remained slow, measured. He kept up a steady stream of conversation with the horse before coming to a stop. He put the lightweight saddle on her. "That didn't hurt, now did it?" With a practiced motion, he swung a leg over the saddle.

Willow accepted his weight with a short whinny, then settled down. Horse and rider circled the corral several times before Cade removed the hood.

George slapped his hat against his thigh. "I've never seen anything like it."

Johanna nodded. "How soon can you start?" she asked Cade when he joined her at the railing once more.

"Today soon enough?"

For the first time, she smiled. "More than all right."

He grinned, the lines at the corners of his eyes deepening. "Thanks."

Now that the introductions were over, Cade took his time in studying Johanna Kellerman. Hair that reminded him of the color of autumn leaves framed a heart-shaped face. Green eyes held intelligence and humor.

Her too-big men's pants were cinched with a heavy belt; circles of sweat darkened the underarms of her shirt. Her hands bore calluses, scratches, and scars.

The lady was no straw boss. He liked that she wasn't afraid to get her hands dirty.

"You're staring," she said.

Caught, he smiled. "Was I? Sorry. I was just wondering how a woman came to be boss of this outfit."

A shadow crossed her face. "I inherited it from my parents." She turned and started to walk away.

He knew there was more to it than that. His reports showed that her adopted father had left her a rundown ranch with few assets and a mountain of debts. The little he'd learned so far about the Double J revealed it was currently well run, respected in the town and surrounding area. Not bad for a small operation. His admiration of the lady went up another notch.

"Miss Kellerman?" he called.

She turned.

"Thanks for the job. You won't be sorry you took me on."

"It's Johanna, and you're welcome." She fixed him with a steady gaze. "I hope you're right."

It wouldn't be any hardship working here, he decided. From what he'd seen so far, it was first-class all the way despite its small size. The animals came first. Johanna might skimp on her own comfort, but the barn was meticulously clean, the hay fresh.

He was impressed—with the Double J and with its owner.

Cade watched as Johanna headed to the stock pens. She walked with an unconscious grace. With a start, he realized whom she reminded him of. Trudy Wingate. A younger, happier Trudy.

Forcibly, he jerked his thoughts back to the job he was here to do. A frown replaced his earlier grin. He didn't like deceiving Johanna. One look at her eyes convinced him she was as honest and open as the Colorado sky.

Right now, though, he didn't like his job very much. In fact, he didn't much like himself.

Then he thought of Noah. He owed his brother. There was no way he'd let Wingate get his claws into him.

Cade slammed his fist into his palm. He would stand by Noah. Whatever it took.

The relief he should have felt upon choosing his course was conspicuously absent. Blood was thicker than water.

## *Chapter Two*

The sun was a fiery ball in the sky, the morning still cool but warming with the promise of the high desert heat. Yellow tufts of grass pocked the rough ground. Ragged-edged mountains surrounded the Double J under a startling blue sky.

For as long as Johanna could remember, the mountains had been the backdrop for her life. They provided a constancy that kept her grounded. Soon the aspens would begin to turn, their leaves a brilliant splash of yellow against the dark green pines. After the leaves had dropped, snow would shroud the mountain peaks, and sunrise would show the rolling expanse of meadows at the foothills to be luminous with frost.

Johanna wondered about the new man who'd shown up two days ago. If Larrabee worked out like she hoped, she'd offer him a permanent job.

She frowned. He didn't look like the kind of man who stayed in one place for long. A drifter? Maybe. Somehow, though, she didn't think so.

Perhaps it was the way he had of looking at a person with eyes so steady and clear that you knew he was a man you could count on. Perhaps it was the quiet but firm way he had with horses. Only a few people possessed that quality, that special affinity with the animals. Her pa was one of them. George was another. And now Cade.

From where she poured feed in a bucket, she watched as Cade polished his saddle. A man who paid that kind of attention to his saddle was likely to give the same attention to his work.

Over the following days, she kept a close watch on Larrabee. He kept to himself for the most part, working quietly and methodically at any job assigned him. He didn't complain at mucking out the stalls, a job given to the newest hired hand. He had an easy manner, but Johanna sensed an underlying seriousness to him.

Any doubts Johanna had concerning his experience had vanished as she watched the comfortable way he handled the animals. Not that he was casual with them—he was too much a professional for that.

He treated the animals with respect, even gentleness. Any animal he worked with received the same attention, whether it be a prize stallion brought to the Double J for training or an aging animal she kept solely out of sentiment. He checked under the girth for sores and made sure that a blanket was used under the saddle.

When quitting time came, Johanna gave an absent wave to the men as they headed to the bunk house.

"You staying on?" George asked.

"I thought I'd start on framing the barn," she said, not looking up from where she was measuring a freshly sawed length of wood.

A new barn would give her the space to board more animals for training. The problem, as always, was time. She couldn't spare the men to work on it during the day, so she tried to squeeze in hours at the end of her day to work on it.

"I'll give you a hand."

She lifted her head. "And risk having Sarah scold me for keeping you late? You get home and take care of her."

"You sure?"

She assumed a fierce glare. "I'm still the boss around here, aren't I?"

He grinned. "Yes, ma'am, you sure 'nough are."

A matching grin curved her lips. "Just so you remember."

She kept at her task, so intent that she didn't hear the sound of boots on the rough floor.

"Could you use another hand?" a voice asked.

Startled, she gave a small gasp.

"Sorry," Cade said. "I didn't mean to scare you."

"It's all right. I just didn't expect . . . I thought everyone had gone."

"The men are playing poker. I'm not much of a card player, so I figured I'd stay and see if you needed some help."

She hesitated. Having another pair of hands would make the work go faster.

"Hey, if it makes you uncomfortable or something, just say so and I'll get out of here."

"No," she said quickly, feeling foolish. "I appreciate the help."

"I saw you chase George off," he said as he held up a

length of wood to be cut. "He'd have stayed if you'd asked him to."

"Yeah."

"Why didn't you?"

"Because he'd have stayed." At the question in his eyes, she said, "He has a wife, and a baby on the way." A wrinkle worked its way between her brows as she sawed her end.

"You care about him."

It wasn't a question, and she didn't treat it as such. "George and Sarah are my friends. They'd do anything for me. That's why I can't ask him."

Cade nodded, as if confirming something to himself.

They worked well together, quickly establishing a rhythm of measuring and sawing.

The hours passed quickly, melting away under Cade's undemanding company.

After several hours, Cade said, "Time for a break."

She was about to refuse when she yawned widely. Her muscles ached with a good kind of hurt, the sort that came with hard work.

"I owe you an apology. This isn't your job. I've kept you longer than I should."

"I volunteered," he reminded her. "You're pushing yourself hard."

"If I can get the framing done before cold weather sets in, I'll have a leg up on finishing before winter comes. That means I'll be able to board more horses, train them, and make a profit."

He sketched a small salute. "We make a good team."

"We do, don't we?"

"Mind if I ask you a question?" he asked as he made

himself comfortable on a length of board stretched across two sawhorses. He patted the spot next to him, and, after a moment's hesitation, she sat down.

"If I do, I'll let you know."

"Why do you keep yourself apart from the rest of the men?"

She stiffened. "Do I?"

"Yeah. You're friendly, but only up to a point. Then you back away. Just like you did this afternoon. With me."

"I didn't—"

His steady gaze silenced the lie she'd been about to utter.

"Okay, maybe I did."

"Why?" he asked bluntly.

"I was never very good at making friends."

"Then we have something in common."

To her relief, he didn't pursue the subject. They resumed their work, completing far more than if she'd been working on her own.

She slid down the wall of a stall and wrapped her arms around her knees. "Thanks. You saved me a late night."

"You're welcome." He stretched out beside her. "You don't give yourself much slack, do you?"

"Can't afford to."

"Don't you ever take a day off?"

Her lips edged upward. "Sure. As soon as the cattle learn to herd themselves and the horses learn to train themselves and the fences learn to mend themselves and—"

He held up his hands. "I get it."

Her smile died. "Yeah. Right now, though, I can't

afford a day off. Not if I want to make my next payment to the bank."

"You push yourself too hard."

"No choice," she said. A seventeen-hour day wasn't unusual. Some nights, when she fell into bed, she imagined she heard her shoulders and arms weeping with fatigue and her feet begging for mercy.

Drowsily, she tried to focus on what he was saying. She felt her eyes close and tried to force them open, but it was too much effort.

"Johanna?"

"Mmm."

Something shook her shoulder. She shrugged it off. She felt strong arms lifting, carrying her. Of course it was a dream. She knew where she was. In a few minutes, she'd get up and head to the house. In the meantime, though, she'd enjoy the sensation of being held against a hard chest.

The dream was alive with details. A breeze whispered over her. She heard a door opening, then closing. Now she was nestling in her bed, felt her boots being removed, a blanket being drawn over her.

"Sleep well," a voice murmured.

When pale streams of light found their way through the window, she groaned and turned over, pulling the pillow over her head.

She checked how high the sun was in the sky and confirmed what she already knew. It was far past the time she should be up. All she wanted to do was crawl back under the covers and stay in bed.

Bed.

She didn't remember going to bed last night. In fact,

she didn't remember much of anything, beside the fact that she and Cade had worked on a wall of the new barn.

Cade!

Had he brought her to the house?

Her face heated with the memory of what she'd thought had been a dream—Cade lifting her, carrying her. Now she knew why it had seemed so real.

The man had seen a need, and seen to it. Nothing to get so het up about. He probably hadn't given it a second thought. Well, neither would she.

Only one flaw marred her resolve. The memory of those strong arms holding her close refused to vanish.

Work filled the following days. She dropped into bed at night exhausted but happy. Framing the new barn was moving along at a rate she had only dared to hope. Part of the reason—a large part, she acknowledged—was Cade. There was nothing he couldn't turn his hand to: training horses, repairing fences, building barns.

She said a silent prayer of thanks that he had found his way to the Double J.

He had quickly made friends among the other ranch hands. Only George remained standoffish.

When Johanna asked her foreman about it, he gave her a noncommittal smile. "I'm still trying to get a handle on him."

His stubborn refusal to accept Cade puzzled her. Still, she couldn't order the men to like one another. As long as they worked together, she wouldn't complain.

"I'm thinking of sending you and Jarvis over to the far meadow," she said. "I'd feel better if we got a head start on the fencing there."

George looked surprised. "I thought the branding came first."

"It does. But that doesn't mean I can afford to tie up everyone on it."

He scratched his head. "Who you going to leave here?"

"Larrabee and Thompson."

He hesitated. "What about you?"

"I'll be working here," she said.

Worry lines worked their way across his forehead. "You sure about Larrabee? I know the man knows his way around horses, but he's still pretty new. You don't know him."

"I know enough. Why don't you trust him?"

"I don't not trust him. That don't mean I trust him, if you catch my meaning."

Johanna caught it all right. And didn't like it. "Has he done anything to make you distrust him?"

"No . . ." George drew the word out, his narrow face creased in thought. "But something doesn't sit right with me. Larrabee's no ordinary ranch hand."

She smiled, relieved. "You're right about that. He's the best trainer I've seen, outside of you and Pa."

"Yeah. But that ain't what I meant."

Exasperated now, she planted her hands on her hips. "Just what do you mean?"

"He's got a fine way with horses. Mighty fine. So why's he working for . . ." His voice trailed off in an embarrassed silence.

"A two-bit outfit like the Double J," she finished for him.

"You run a first-class place," George said quickly.

"You know that. But I can't help wondering about Larrabee. He could work for any of the bigger spreads, but he picks here."

She'd wondered the same thing. Right now, though, she needed him too much to question her good luck in his turning up. "Anything else bothering you?"

George shook his head. "I'm just looking out for you, the way your pa would have wanted me to."

She reached up to kiss his cheek. "I know. And I thank you for it."

George was the closest thing she had to family. He didn't have much schooling, but he knew more about people—and horses—than anyone she knew. If he said something didn't seem right about Cade Larrabee, she ought to listen.

For the first time she could remember, though, she ignored George's advice. She needed Cade for the skill he brought to the job, but honesty compelled her to admit it was more than that. She liked him and wondered what it would feel like to have him hold her hand, even kiss her.

She shoved her hair back from her forehead and laughed at herself. Since when had she started thinking of Cade beauing her? He'd probably be embarrassed to death if he learned of her fantasies. She liked him. That wasn't hard to understand. Aside from being the best-looking man she'd come across in ages, Cade was also intelligent and sensitive. She had the feeling that he'd understand what she wanted to do with the Double J, her need to make it a success.

By dusk, she was ready to call it a day. The rest of the hands had already left. As she started toward the house, she spotted a flickering light in the barn.

More exasperated than concerned, she headed in that direction. Probably George, trying to get a head start on tomorrow's work. She'd chew him out and send him on his way. She knew he was worried about the work piling up, but she couldn't allow him to work evenings as well as days. Sarah would have her hide.

The lecture she planned to deliver was forgotten as she saw Cade stacking bags of feed. She didn't bother with words but grabbed a bag and started with it toward the far wall.

"You shouldn't be doing that."

"More hands make light work," Johanna said lightly.

"Yeah." Cade let out the word in a grunt of effort. He had to admire Johanna's pluck. She couldn't have weighed much over one hundred pounds, but she managed to hold her own. She knew how to lift, using her legs instead of her back.

"Look," she said after they worked an hour, "I appreciate your staying late to finish up, but I can't let you work all night."

He lifted a shoulder in a half-shrug. "It's got to be done."

"I appreciate it," she repeated. "But it's not right. You put in a full day as it is."

"Hey, I like doing it. Are you going to scold me for liking my work?"

Put like that, she couldn't very well object. "You win." Realizing how ungracious she must have sounded, she smiled. "I really do appreciate it."

"You're welcome." He seemed anxious to drop the subject and brushed a smudge of dirt from her cheek.

"By the way, I'm thinking of sending the rest of the men over to the south meadow."

"Everyone?"

"Everyone but you, me, and Thompson. He's the best when it comes to wielding a branding iron. You and I can take care of the castration. I think between us we can finish up."

"You're the boss."

The easy camaraderie between them suffused her with warmth as she got ready for bed that night. Cade Larrabee was fast becoming important to her. Maybe too important.

She clamped down on her self-recriminations with a force that surprised her. She was twenty-seven years old, after all. There was nothing wrong in finding a man attractive.

"C'mon," she said to Cade the following morning. "We still have half a herd to send through the chute."

"Yes, ma'am," Cade called.

They passed a dozen steers through the chute. Cade had to hand it to Johanna. She worked her men hard, but no harder than herself. She wrestled a reluctant steer with an ease that belied her small size.

Sweat sheened her skin, darkened her rough men's shirt. She swiped a hand across her forehead but didn't stop.

When she looked ready to drop from exhaustion, he put up a hand. "Hold on. You've got more work lined up than ten men can do. You can't expect to finish it with just the two of us."

"If it's too much for you—"

"It's not me I'm worrying about."

The quiet concern in his voice gave her pause. "I'll pull some men off another job when we need them. But I'm hoping we can handle the next few days by ourselves."

"Are things that bad?"

"No . . . not really. Only I can't pay any more men right now."

"Listen, if it'd help, I can get by without this month's wages. I can wait until things are better."

He watched as her spine turned rigid, her posture as stiff as a soldier's, her expression as hard and deadly as a warrior readying for battle.

Then she relaxed. "That's really decent of you, Cade. But things aren't that bad. When it gets to where I can't pay my men, it's time to close up."

He guessed he'd offended her sense of pride. He understood pride, and had a healthy dose of it himself. "You're a special lady, Johanna Kellerman."

She smiled, though it had a forced quality to it.

He frowned, wondering what was wrong. "Did I say something wrong?"

"No . . . it's just my pa used to call me his 'little lady.' I haven't thought of that in over a year. Not since he died."

He chanced a touch to her cheek. "I'm sorry. I didn't mean to bring back memories."

"Don't apologize. They're good memories. I keep them stored away so I can take them out and relive them." She laughed. "Sometimes I think I store them away too much." She looked at him curiously. "Do you store away memories too?"

Cade thought about it and then nodded slowly. "I guess I do."

"Do you ever take them out and look at them again?"

"No." He didn't qualify his answer. Some memories hurt too much to examine. Better to let them stay buried.

"Oh." She bit her lip.

"Hey, it's okay," he said to cover the awkward silence. He couldn't stem the tide of memories, though. Rather than fight them, he let them have their way.

When his mother had died, his father had retreated into a shell of his own. The family that had been his for a short six years was no longer. He and Noah had quickly learned to fend for themselves.

When Cade's father should have been holding onto his sons, he'd held onto a bottle instead. His paltry earnings—from the mines, where he'd worked for more than twenty years—more often than not went to whiskey.

For more nights than Cade cared to remember, he and Noah had gone to bed hungry. He could still hear his cries on those nights when darkness closed around him, the memories returning as a bad dream to haunt him with undiminished power.

At seventeen, Noah was practically supporting Cade and himself with odd jobs he'd picked up at neighboring ranches. He'd sworn they'd never go to bed hungry again.

After Noah joined the army, he'd sent most of his pay home. Cade had a bad case of hero worship back then. When Noah had signed up, Cade could hardly wait until he was old enough to join.

Things changed when Noah came home minus his legs, but it hadn't dimmed Cade's dream of being a soldier. On the contrary, he was more determined than ever to wear blue and serve the Union.

After the war, he'd followed the general west.

Since then, he'd discovered he was good at what he did. Little gave him more satisfaction than going into a tense situation, defusing it, and restoring order. He'd advanced until he'd become the general's number one man, called in when no one else could get the job done.

Getting the job done. That was all that mattered. Protecting Noah was the only thing that mattered, the only thing that *could* matter.

When Sage came down with colic late one evening, Johanna dropped everything. Nothing mattered as much as her old friend.

She had learned to ride on Sage's back. Later, she'd needed a more spirited horse, but she'd never forgotten Sage. When the mare became too old for day-long rides through the desert, Johanna still visited her, never failing to bring an apple or carrot.

To Johanna's horror, Sage lay down and rolled from side to side. Unlike sheep and cattle, horses didn't whimper when they were in pain. Instead, Sage strained to look at her belly, as though to ask for help.

Johanna knew the danger if the stomach ruptured. Sage would die.

Sweat coated the mare's neck and flanks. The pleading in her eyes pulled at Johanna's heart.

Cade showed up, lines of worry creasing his face. "George told me what happened. How can I help?"

She basked in the genuine concern in his voice, but the

offer of help nearly undid her. "She can't get up . . . if a horse doesn't get up . . ." She didn't finish. She didn't have to. Her voice wobbled, a shaky, quivery sound she hated because of the weakness it betrayed.

She shifted her gaze away from his, but not in time to hide the moisture in her eyes.

His hands slid up her arms and came to rest on her shoulders. She fought the temptation to lean on him, if only for a moment.

He ignored her resistance and wound his arms around her waist to draw her close. She melted against his chest and let him hold her. The surprise of it raced through her. When was the last time she'd allowed herself to lean on someone else?

Then came other surprises, one on top of another. The feel of being held against a man's strong chest. The scent of leather and male. And soap. He actually smelled of lye soap. Not many men of her acquaintance bathed. Even her pa, the finest man she'd ever known, declared bathing was something only womenfolk did.

A weak whinny from Sage turned her thoughts back to more important matters, but she stored the information about Cade away, something to take out and examine later.

He pressed his lips to her hair. "It's going to be all right," he murmured, the words barely audible. But she caught them and the concern behind them.

"Do you have any ginger beer?" Cade asked.

"I think I could scare up some. What are you planning on doing with it?"

"An old remedy I learned back when I was growing up."

She hurried to the house and returned within a few minutes with the ginger beer.

Cade took a powder from his saddlebags and mixed it with the ginger beer. Between the two of them, they got the liquid down Sage's throat.

After a few minutes, Sage stumbled to her feet. Johanna knew better than to think their troubles were over. She and Cade took turns walking Sage, back and forth, back and forth, their pace matching hers.

Dusk deepened into night, and still they continued working over the mare.

When Sage refused to take another step and collapsed on the barn floor, Johanna felt her heart—and hopes—plummet.

Cade produced a couple of blankets. Johanna's eyes filled with fresh tears at the care he showed for her. At the same time, it sent a funny sensation dancing over her skin.

"Come on," he said. "We might as well get comfortable."

"You don't have to stay," she said, hearing the quiver in her voice. Though she dreaded the thought of the long hours spent alone, standing vigil over Sage, she couldn't expect Cade to understand how much her old friend meant to her. Or to spend the night in a cold, drafty barn.

Cade took her hands and pressed them between his own. "I'm staying."

She looked at him, his features slightly blurred in the dim light from the oil lamp. "I'm not used to taking help from anyone. In case you haven't noticed, I'm not very good at it. And I'm not comfortable with it." The shakes, she noted, had smoothed out of her voice.

Another reason, a more important one, kept her from

accepting his offer. His nearness made her nerves quiver, her pulse pound. She curled her lower lip between her teeth, more unsettled by his closeness than she wanted to admit.

He caught her jaw in the V between his thumb and fingers, giving her no choice but to look at him. "I'm not asking. I'm just doing it, so don't think you've got a choice in the matter."

Cade had an idea of how much Sage meant to her, how she'd blame herself if the mare didn't pull through. So much pain was etched in her face. He wanted to take it away, to make everything right for her.

He looked down at her tear-stained cheeks, lifting her chin with his forefinger when she tried to pull away. Something moved inside him, something oddly compelling. Unable to help himself, he lowered his head; knowing it was wrong didn't prevent him from cupping her face and kissing her. Gently. Tenderly.

When the kiss ended, she reached for his hand and laced her fingers through his.

Cade felt the gentle warmth, the comfort in her touch. He was the one who was supposed to do the comforting.

He took another look at her face, frowning at what he saw there. The gray cast to her skin worried him. How long had it been since she'd had anything to eat?

"I'll get you something to eat," he said.

She thanked him with a tired smile that didn't reach her eyes.

Returning a few minutes later with a kettle of tea and sandwiches, he found Johanna checking on Sage.

"She's breathing easier now."

He heard the note of cautious optimism in her voice,

the hope that wouldn't quit despite the odds against the mare's recovery. He nodded, noting the steady rise and fall of Sage's sides. He dropped to the floor, propping his back against the rough wood of the stall. "Come here," he said, patting the spot beside him.

She hesitated only a moment before dropping to the ground. Together, they ate the food neither wanted. Once they'd finished, he pulled her to him, settling her into the shelter of his arms.

He shifted so that her head rested comfortably against his shoulder. When he pulled a blanket over her, she frowned.

"I can't go to sleep," she protested. "I have to stay awake and watch over her."

"I know. But there's no sense being uncomfortable."

She nodded, her eyes drifting shut until she snapped them open. He smiled to himself. She fought her exhaustion as she fought anything that stood in her way. He could see the struggle on her face.

Within a few minutes, she slipped into sleep. He felt her every shift and sigh, the sound little more than a soft shifting of air, as she nestled against him. Gently, he pulled off her boots and tucked the blanket around her.

She seemed younger and more vulnerable as sleep softened the stubborn set of her jaw. Incredibly long lashes, tipped with the same gold as her hair, rested upon her cheeks. To soothe them both, he gave in to the temptation to brush his lips against her forehead. She stirred but didn't waken.

With Johanna curled at his side, he was reminded how small she was, how delicate. He could easily encircle her wrist with his thumb and forefinger and still have room left over. "Delicate" wasn't a word he normally associated with her. She was so vibrant, so full of energy and life that he forgot just how little she really was.

He reached for her hand. Calluses pocked the pale gold skin. The life of a rancher wasn't for the weak or faint-hearted. She didn't let her size keep her from doing her job, though. He'd seen her tackle jobs that would intimidate men twice her size. She had more grit than anyone he'd ever met.

He'd never felt that way about any woman before, and it brought a ripple of panic to his chest.

Realizing just where his thoughts were taking him, he frowned. He didn't need that kind of complication in his life. He was fighting to shield his brother. A woman like Johanna was bound to interfere with that. He had to concentrate on what had brought him to the Double J in the first place.

She started in her sleep, the reflexive jerk causing her fingers to tense around his. He soothed them with his thumb, until she relaxed once again. He kept her hand in his, finding the clasp oddly comforting.

Sage turned her head to stare at him, her chocolate brown eyes seeming to ask his intentions. "It's okay, girl. I'll take care of her."

Johanna awoke to the sound of gentle whickering. She turned her head to watch Sage eating from her feed box. Only then did Johanna realize that she was curled in Cade's arms. Gently, she freed herself, careful not to wake him.

A wave of warmth washed over her as she recalled

the genuine worry in his eyes last night, his unflagging energy in caring for Sage.

She stood unsteadily, her legs numb from the long hours on the cold floor, but the discomfort couldn't dim her elation over seeing Sage standing.

"Sage." Johanna wrapped her arms around the mare's neck and received a nuzzle in return.

Giving an impatient snort, Sage stuck her head in her feed box once more.

"Hey, girl," Johanna murmured, rubbing the mare's neck. "You gave us a real scare, but you're going to be all right. Not too much at once," she said when the mare kept right on eating.

The crunch of Sage's huge teeth chomping on her feed was music to Johanna ears. She nudged the animal aside and laughed when Sage tried to nip her.

After assuring herself that Sage wasn't going to overeat, Johanna stretched and wiped her eyes. Her nose wrinkled as she caught a whiff of herself. After twenty-four hours in the same clothes and sleeping in the barn, she smelled like one of the animals.

Sage kept down her food and was now fretting to go for a run.

"Not yet," Johanna said, her hands gentle as she groomed the mare. The repetitious motion smoothed away the rough edges left by a night spent in a barn stall, soothing her as well as her old friend.

Sage responded with a soft whinny.

Johanna gave her a final pat and led her outside. With a pat to the mare's rump, she let Sage go. Sage took off at a trot for the far corner of the corral. The sight of her running filled Johanna with joy. Only the day before, Sage had been down, giving every appearance of never being able to get up again.

Dawn speared pink fingers of light through the cloud-laden sky. Johanna looked up, hoping the clouds meant rain. Like most country folk, she followed the weather. The county had been too long without moisture, and draught conditions were ripe, but little could ruin her mood this morning.

Though she'd been raised here, Johanna never tired of the sunrises, the colors so brilliant to rival that of the most spectacular scenery in the world. Dotted with cacti and inhabited by scorpions and gila monsters, the land was as harsh and unforgiving as the climate, but it held its own beauty. And she wouldn't trade it for all the lush greenery in the world.

She swiped her hands down her legs, managing to dislodge some of the dirt and straw that clung to her but none of the smell.

"That's not going to help much."

She spun around to find Cade watching her. He smiled, a slow, gut-wrenching look that went all the way to her toes and then back again. In that heartbeat of time, she knew this man was someone who could matter to her, matter a great deal.

With a start, she realized how she must look. She put a hand to her hair and tried to smooth it into some kind of order.

"Don't. You're beautiful."

The man was crazy. Or blind. How else could she explain his ridiculous observation?

She stared at him. A day's growth of beard shadowed his jaw. His eyes were blurry with fatigue. And she wanted very much for him to kiss her just as he'd kissed her last night.

As though he had read her thoughts, he was at her side in two long strides. "There's something I've been wanting to do ever since last night."

When he moved his hand to cup her neck, she knew what was coming. The intent in his eyes was obvious, as was the shortness of his breath. Gently, so very gently, he fitted his lips to hers. He deepened the kiss, shaping his mouth against hers. It was a meeting of lips but so much more. Giving and taking.

She concentrated on breathing. Breathing in and breathing out. She gave herself up to the kiss, hungry for his touch.

He was the one to break the sweet contact, to raise his head and smile.

When he raised his head, he was shaken. The kiss wasn't supposed to have been anything but a quick caress. It had taken him by surprise. He hadn't expected it. Least of all did he expect his reaction to it.

"I'm sorry." He felt as awkward as a schoolboy caught kissing his best girl in the school yard.

"Don't apologize. I enjoyed it."

Her honesty startled him almost as much as the kiss. She was as guileless as a child, with her huge eyes gazing straight into his heart. He urged her to him, his hands resting at her waist.

He forgot that he was here for a few weeks only, a month at the most. He forgot that Johanna was a job, that he had no place for a woman in his life. He forgot everything, everything but the woman in his arms.

He didn't try to kiss her again. He was content to

hold her, to feel her heart beat a rapid rhythm against his chest. Words were unnecessary, which was good, because he couldn't think of a thing to say.

His fingers brushed hers.

Johanna snatched her hand away and then flushed. There was no need to feel flustered, no reason for the tingling awareness that shivered up her arm. Still, she couldn't stem the color that she knew was flooding her face.

He gestured to the horse who was now chewing straw contentedly. "You're a special lady, Johanna."

Pleasure at his words heightened the color in her already pink cheeks.

"Last night . . . thank you. For everything." Did that stammering bit of nonsense come from her? She was remembering how it felt to have his arms around her, his lips a scant inch from her own.

"You're welcome, but you've already thanked me. More than once."

For a moment, she imagined she knew what he was thinking. He didn't smile, didn't make a move toward her, but something in the depth of his gaze told her that he too was remembering what it felt like to hold her, to kiss her.

What was she doing? She'd known the man a scant few days, but she felt a sense of rightness with him, about him.

She found herself recalling a conversation with her mother many years ago, when Johanna had had her heart broken by a boy at school.

"I'm never going to fall in love again," Johanna had wailed.

Jenny Kellerman had laughed gently. "You will. And someday it will be with the right man. At the right time."

Was Cade that man?

She stared up at him, taking in the strength in his jaw, the rangy length of his body. He was a large man whom she'd known for less than a week. The only things she knew were what he'd told her, and every word of it could be a lie.

She was twenty-seven years old and had never been in love. What did she know about men, about anything?

Common sense told her to take things slowly where this man was concerned, but her heart told her different.

## *Chapter Three*

From the moment he'd touched his lips to hers, things felt awkward between them. The way he looked at her. The way he noticed her looking at him. Something had shifted between them, and it sorely tested Cade's resolve to keep his distance.

Johanna brushed his cheek, her hand soft and warm. It wasn't soft in the way of the pampered hands of the women he met at the few social functions he'd attended. Their hands had never known the calluses that came from hard work.

No, hers was soft in the way it touched his face, soft in the way it soothed away the pain of the past, soft in the way it gave comfort.

For those reasons and more, Cade jerked away.

"I'm sorry," she murmured, flushing.

He tried a smile. "It's okay. You startled me." He couldn't explain why he'd jumped as if he'd been scalded. She wouldn't understand. He wasn't sure he did.

Softness had no place in his life. Then why did he

respond with such startling intensity to the touch of a woman's hand? Especially this woman's hand? A woman he was sent to watch, to spy upon.

As a child, his only means of survival had been a strong body and a fierce determination. Serving in the Union army, he'd honed his body and skills, ignoring the softer side of his nature.

Since his ma's death, nothing in his life had prepared him to accept gentleness or compassion. So long had he been without them that he didn't know how to deal with them when they were offered. So he made it a rule to avoid them.

Oh, he had softer feelings. He wasn't the cold-blooded hired gun Wingate and others thought him. He'd deliberately cultivated that image, having found it useful in his line of work, but he'd learned early on to keep his more tender feelings under wraps. They made a man vulnerable, something he couldn't afford.

Instead of maintaining his objectivity, he'd allowed his emotions to drop him into the middle of her life. At that moment, all he wanted was to do the job and get out of there.

Distance was the key word here. As long as he maintained a professional distance from Johanna, he'd be all right.

With an effort, he brought himself back to the present. The harshness around his mouth disappeared, and he heard Johanna draw a relieved breath.

He was close to letting the job become personal, and that was a big mistake. He had a job to do, he reminded himself. He had to stay fixed on that, had to concentrate on protecting his brother, not Johanna, however appealing he found her.

Now he wondered about her reaction to him. Did she share the attraction he felt? The idea pleased him until he realized its implications. He'd do well to remember that he was here to do a job, not fall in love with the pretty boss.

The acknowledgement tainted his mouth with bitterness.

He swiped at his forehead with the back of his hand, then stripped off his shirt. His chest and shoulders, bronzed brown by the sun, glistened under a fine sheen of sweat.

Johanna couldn't help but notice his hard muscles, and she flushed as she realized that his eyes had followed the direction of her gaze.

When he turned his back to her, she saw it. A thin scar ran from under his arm to disappear beneath the waistband of his pants, a white slash against dark gold skin. She wanted to ask him about it but thought better of it. Another scar bisected his shoulder.

Finished with his task, Cade picked up his shirt. "Hope you don't mind that I shed my shirt. It's hotter than a . . ." He grinned. "It's plenty hot."

"I don't mind," she said, still thinking about the scar. "Uh . . . I . . ."

"What?"

"Nothing."

"Would nothing be the scar you were staring at?"

"How did you know?"

"I've lived with that little souvenir for over twelve

years. Let's just say I'm accustomed to people's reactions."

There was nothing she could say to that. "I'm sorry."

"For staring?"

She shook her head. "That you were hurt."

His gaze bored into her until she flushed uncomfortably. "You mean that, don't you?"

"Yes."

Her voice was but a thread of sound, but it must have registered, for he nodded briefly.

Tentatively, she reached out. When he didn't flinch, her wandering fingers found and paused at the scar on his shoulder. She felt him tremble beneath her touch and then go still.

He held himself motionless, as though she were hurting him all over again. Reason told her she wasn't, she was making her exploration as gentle as possible, but she couldn't help the hiss of breath that escaped her lips as she brought her hand away.

He wouldn't have been surprised to find the scars had disappeared completely when she removed her hand, so soothing was her touch, so gentle her probing fingers. This woman gave comfort as easily as she breathed. Everything in him clamored to take what she offered. At the same time, everything revolted against accepting it. He didn't deserve her compassion.

She turned questioning eyes up to his. "Was it bad?" Stupid question, she scolded herself. Of course it had been bad. She had only to look at the network of scars to know the wounds must have brought him close to death.

"War has no winners, only losers."

"Were you wounded more than once?"

He saw the compassion in her face. Her eyes were tender with caring, plain for him to see. Unguarded.

He'd also heard the concern in her voice, a concern she hadn't tried to conceal. Johanna was too honest to hide what she felt behind a protective armor. He saw the pain in her eyes. The feeling it roused in him startled him. He'd expected to be annoyed; instead, he felt warmed. How long had it been since someone—anyone—had truly cared about him?

The answer came with cruel swiftness. No one but Noah cared whether he lived or died. A long time to live with the knowledge that it would hardly raise a ripple in the world if he died.

"A few times."

She gave a moan of anguish. Slowly, her hands traveled across the firm muscles of his lower back, finding two more scars. Tears gathered in her eyes at the thought of his suffering.

He touched a finger to the glistening wetness on her cheeks. "Don't cry for me, honey. It was a long time ago."

"But you were all alone."

"No. There were others." A contraction of pain twisted his face as he remembered friends who hadn't made it home.

"But no one who cared what happened to you," she guessed, remembering how alone he seemed.

"I was one of the lucky ones."

"Lucky," she scoffed.

"I was," he insisted, uncomfortable with her compassion. "I came home all in one piece, which is more than a lot of men did. More than my . . ." He didn't finish, even when she glanced at him, questions clear in her eyes.

Memories crowded his mind, memories he thought he'd put to rest long ago. And, within that space of time, from one moment to the next, he was transported back to the battleground, where only fate decided who would live and who would die.

He recalled a credo from one of the books his ma had read to him and Noah over the years: *Draw me not without reason. Sheathe me not without honor.* Below the words was a drawing of a pair of crossed swords.

The words had steadied him in the chaos of war.

He'd watched his friends die, watched the enemy die, until death surrounded him, until death was all there was. The sights, the sounds, the smells were forever imprinted upon his mind, his soul. The ringing in his ears. Heart racing so fast that it seemed it would surely burst right out of his chest, blood pumping too rapidly, sweat oozing from his pores.

And the sickly sweet odor of blood overriding everything else.

It caught him off guard how easily he had confided in her, feelings he had never shared with anyone, until now.

"I wish there weren't any wars," she said at last when it became plain he didn't intend on finishing whatever it was he'd been about to say.

He nodded shortly. "So do I. Okay if I wash up at the trough?"

"Sure." She watched as he dunked a dipper in the trough, then poured it over himself. Obviously he didn't wish to continue the conversation. She wouldn't press him, though she longed to know what he wasn't telling her.

Johanna felt the pressure of tears build behind her eyes. Something about this man saddened her. It was more than the scars slashing his skin, a mute reminder of a painful past. It was the aloofness he withdrew into whenever she got too close. Loneliness like that was painful to see. It touched her down to her very soul.

An uneasy expression had crossed his face at her questions—almost frightened, but only for a moment. He was good at covering his feelings. Maybe a little too good. It was almost as if he were accustomed to hiding what he felt, what he thought.

She sighed and shelved the idea. Maybe she was entirely wrong about him. Maybe he kept to himself because he preferred it that way. She shook her head, remembering the bleakness in his eyes when he'd talked of his past. No, she wasn't mistaken. He wanted, needed, someone capable of understanding, of caring about him.

A frisson of uneasiness ruffled her heart. There were so many things about him she didn't know, and even more that she didn't understand. Cade Larrabee had more than his share of secrets—secrets he had no intention of sharing with her.

The kind of togetherness her heart longed for left no room for secrets. Since when had she started thinking of Cade in those terms? She gave herself a mental shake.

A shiver danced down her spine as a new thought came to her. Did one of those secrets concern her?

Where had that thought come from? The result of an overactive imagination, she decided, her lips curving in a faint smile. Her pa had teased her about her runaway imagination more than once.

Whatever had brought Cade to the Double J, Johanna could only be grateful. Though he'd been here only two weeks, he'd accomplished a great deal. They were ahead of schedule on framing the addition to the barn. A few more weeks should see it finished.

The men deserved a reward for all their hard work. The idea took shape in her mind. A party, with wives and children invited.

She suggested the idea to George when he rode over from the south meadow.

He grinned broadly. "The men'll love it. When were you thinking?"

"Saturday night."

"Uh, Boss?"

"Hmm?"

"Can you afford a shindig? I know money's tight."

She nodded. "We'll keep things simple."

The news of a party had boosted everyone's morale. Spirits were high by Saturday night.

She took extra care with her appearance, choosing her one skirt and shirtwaist in place of her usual men's pants and shirt. After dabbing lemon verbena—a birthday present from her pa shortly before he died—behind her ears, she decided she was ready.

Would Cade like her in a skirt? The question unnerved her. It had been a long time since she'd cared if a man found her attractive.

Impatient with her foolishness, she pushed the doubts aside and headed outside.

A banner of stars spangled the night sky. For the first

time she could remember, Johanna thought briefly about making a wish upon one. Her practical side took over, and she rejected the idea, but not without a pang of regret.

Hearing fiddle music and laughter, Johanna felt the burden of running the ranch slip from her shoulders, at least for tonight. She visited with the wives and children of her men. Knowing Cade's gaze followed her every movement didn't hurt either.

When the fiddler started in on a reel, she gave herself up to the pleasure of dancing. Her feet moved to the familiar strains of the toe-tapping music. Laughing, she grabbed the hands of her partner and skipped through the tunnel made of hands clasped overhead.

The music ended, and, gratefully, she made her way to the side. She fanned her face with her hand. A cup of lemonade was put in the other.

She looked up to find Cade smiling at her. "Thanks." Her skin was flushed, dotted with perspiration. She knew she must look a sight, but she was having too good a time to care.

He tucked a wayward strand of hair behind her ear. "Dance with me?" he asked when the music slowed to a waltz.

Her stomach fluttered with anticipation as he slipped an arm around her waist and gathered one of her hands against his chest.

She felt enfolded by him, enveloped in a sweet warmth she'd never before experienced. Settling into his embrace, she gave herself up to the moment. The black velvet sky provided the perfect canopy as the evening air cooled her overheated skin.

The music stopped, but he continued to hold her. Imperceptibly, his hold tightened, bringing her closer to him until only a fraction of an inch separated them. What she read in his eyes thrilled and confused her in turn.

"Hey, Boss, great party," Jarvis called, startling her out of the spell the music and Cade's embrace had cast over her. She felt his hands drop away from her sides.

Her throat turned dry. She needed to think, needed to put some distance between her and Cade, was desperate to get herself out of range of those too-perceptive eyes.

"Thank you for the dance." She turned back to Cade, but he was gone.

She looked for him, but he must have left. Struggling against her disappointment, she joined in a square dance and tried to wipe the memory of the kiss from her mind.

It was easier to think about the ranch, about George and Sarah's soon-to-be-born baby, about anything than what had just happened. The distraction worked for a while until she was alone.

She needed time to think about Cade and what was happening between them. She couldn't do that when she was with him. His very presence turned her brain to cornmeal mush.

After saying good-bye to everyone and cleaning up, she headed to the house. She took her time preparing for bed, her thoughts unsettled.

That Cade wasn't an ordinary man, she'd already admitted. That he had the power to slip past the barriers she'd so carefully erected, she still had to acknowledge.

The man had turned her feelings inside out and her life upside down.

As she drifted between wakefulness and sleep, she

puzzled over her response to Cade. She'd shared dances and embraces with men before, but none had touched her the way Cade's had. None had her longing for more. None had left her trembling.

Hours later, when the moon cast silvery fingers of light across the bunkhouse, Cade berated himself.

What had possessed him to dance with Johanna, to hold her as he'd done? He wasn't given to making promises, spoken or unspoken. Promises, even silent ones, had a way of leading to trouble, especially when restlessness nipped at him.

Without effort, he conjured up Johanna's image in his mind. Small and slender, with a delicate bone structure, she reminded him of a finely bred filly. Her already pale skin, stretched tautly over her cheekbones, had been made almost translucent under the moonlight.

In spite of Johanna's fragile appearance, Cade sensed a hidden strength about her that said she would meet whatever hardships she faced.

Resolutely, he put her out of his mind and tried to go to sleep. Two hours later, he gave it up, his thoughts continually straying to the woman who was fast becoming the most important thing in his life.

Why he should feel that way when he barely knew the woman baffled him. Repeatedly he told himself he wasn't interested in her.

He'd met her only a short time ago, but he felt he'd known her far longer. She had been in his thoughts, his blood, ever since he'd first laid eyes on her.

"Who are you, Johanna?" he asked the night. The

sound of the wind in the trees, rhythmic, lulling, was his only answer.

He couldn't shake his desire to wipe away the hurt that he read in her eyes and spare her further pain. That he could be the instrument to inflict the pain tore at his insides with a gut-wrenching pang.

He still hadn't come to terms with the idea that he was deceiving her. She wasn't his concern, but knowing that and accepting it were two entirely different things. His conscience was exacting a price upon him for living a lie.

Suddenly his reason for being here sounded pretty thin. The woman who'd built up her own business, who cared about an out-of-work laborer, wasn't the type to take advantage of an ailing woman.

Johanna Kellerman was an intriguing combination of independence and vulnerability, strength and compassion. He had no right to care about her, Cade reminded himself. He couldn't care. He couldn't afford the distraction.

Getting close to her was only a job. He wondered whom he was trying to fool.

Cade and Johanna had taken to sharing lunch together. He had come to look forward to that time.

In the shade of a huge pine that flanked the house, she poked through the basket and pulled out a sandwich. "I don't know about you, but I'm starved."

He took the sandwich she offered him and bit into it. Roast beef.

She took a bite of apple, and laughed when tart juice squirted in her face.

Her laughter rippled over him, a soft caress of happiness that had been missing from his life for too long. So accustomed had he become to his solitary existence that he'd forgotten how good it felt to simply share ordinary activities such as taking a meal together.

His plan to get to know Johanna better was working out better than he'd dared hope. Everything he learned about her convinced him she was exactly what she appeared to be: honest, hardworking, and blessed with a generous heart.

He told himself that getting close to her was part of his cover, but it was becoming far more than that. He had a rule about getting involved with anyone he met on the job.

The rule had served him well through the years, and he had no intention of breaking it, had never even been tempted to break it. Until now.

He knew better, but Johanna Kellerman tempted him as no woman had in more years than he cared to remember. Something about her had him thinking about things he'd thought he'd put aside: a wife, a home, a house full of children.

Dreams he'd given up on long ago.

Strange how this woman could revive hopes he thought he'd buried a lifetime ago. But then he'd never met a woman like Johanna, never felt this way before, never known it could be this way.

He reminded himself why he was here. As soon as he learned everything he could about Johanna and reported back to the general, the sooner he could leave and get back to his life.

Why did that life suddenly seem so empty? He ignored that and focused on the present.

"Tell me about your parents." He knew most of her history, but he wanted to hear it from her.

"My parents—the Kellermans—adopted me. A missionary couple came through the area and said they'd been asked to place me with a good family."

He waited.

"They were so good to me. They told me I was extra special because I was chosen." Her eyes took on a faraway look. "I wanted to believe them. And I did." She bit her lip and looked away briefly.

"There's more, isn't there?"

"The Kellermans loved me. But I always wondered why my mother—the woman who bore me—didn't." She lifted a shoulder in a negligent shrug. The gesture, meant, he was certain, to convey indifference, revealed a world of hurt instead.

The pain in her voice tore at him, and he ached for the child who believed she'd been rejected by her own mother. He longed to tell her the truth, that Trudy had desperately wanted her.

"It turned out for the best. The Kellermans were wonderful to me," she said. "My mother died five years ago. Pa was never the same after that. He went last year. The doctor said his heart just gave out."

"You don't think so?"

A sad smile slipped across her lips. "I think he died of a broken heart."

"I'm sorry," he said, knowing how inadequate the words sounded, yet unable to say anything else.

"It's all right. I'm glad they're together again. They weren't meant to be apart. They loved each other so much." Her voice caught on the pain of memory.

"And you."

She swiped at her eyes. "That's right. I have great memories. That's more than some people ever have."

He brushed away a tear that had trickled down her cheek. "You still miss them."

"Yeah. I do."

"Tell me a story about them."

"Why?"

"Because memories are good. They make us remember the happy times."

She didn't say anything right away. So many memories. So much laughter. And, in the end, during her mother's long illness, so many tears. A well of emotion pressed against her chest.

"Ma always wanted me to learn to do what she called 'women's work.' Churning butter, making jam, weaving. She tried. Bless her heart, she tried. She tried real hard. But I was never any good at it."

Her mother, one quarter Cherokee, had woven blankets, her nimble fingers creating intricate designs. Instinctively, she'd known what colors to use, what warp and woof would achieve the most beautiful motif.

She had wanted to pass down the tradition to Johanna. To her chagrin, Johanna showed no talent for weaving. Or quilting. Or canning fruits and vegetables. Or any of the other skills women were supposed to have.

In exasperation, her ma had thrown her hands in the air. "Go," she said. "Go to the barn and work with the horses."

Johanna had tried to look regretful but failed miserably, earning an indulgent smile.

"Your heart belongs outside, with the animals. Go. Tell your pa that you will help him."

From that moment, Johanna and her father had been inseparable. Whether it was milking the cows or putting up fence, she turned her hand to it.

Without realizing it, she found herself sharing the memory with Cade. "Pa was glad to have me. He taught me everything I know about running a ranch. But I wish I could have been what Ma wanted."

"I think you were everything she ever wanted," he said softly.

It was the nicest compliment she'd ever received. "What about you, Cade?"

He drew his hand away. "What about me?"

"What kind of memories do you have?"

He thought about it. There were good times, back before his ma died. "The regular childhood memories." He shrugged. "Nothing special."

"Maybe someday you'll trust me enough to tell me."

"It's not that—"

She put a finger to his lips. "When you're ready, I'll be here."

He wondered if she knew what she was offering, if she'd offer so sweetly to listen when it came time to tell her the truth about why he was here.

Bringing her hand to his lips, he kissed her fingers, one by one.

She resisted the urge to pull away. She'd never been self-conscious about her hands before. Callused and scarred, they bore the marks of a lifetime of working with animals. Now, though, she wished they were smooth and soft and feminine, like those of a lady. When he lifted her palm to his mouth, she flinched.

"Don't," he said, apparently guessing her thoughts. "Your hands are beautiful. Like the rest of you."

Her laugh had a forced sound to it. "You're not very observant," she said, finally giving in to the need to shield her hands from his gaze and clenched them together. "I know my hands are ugly."

He took both hands in his, turning the palms up. "I see hard work and pride in that work. That's nothing to be ashamed of."

There was no doubting the sincerity in his voice. Then why couldn't she accept it?

"You don't believe me."

"I do. It's just that I'm not used to—"

"Compliments?"

She nodded, her cheeks flaming to bright red. Sweet heaven, she was blushing. At the advanced age of twenty-seven, she'd thought she'd outgrown the tendency to color up at pretty words.

"Maybe you've been seeing the wrong men."

"Maybe I have." The truth was she hadn't been seeing any men at all, at least not in the way he meant. Most men weren't interested in a woman who worked sixteen hours a day and smelled of manure and sweat. They wanted someone who was there for them at the end of the day with a hot meal and soothing words, someone who wore satin and lace rather than men's trousers and mud-caked boots.

Uncomfortable with where her thoughts were heading, she said, "We ought to get back to work."

"Not yet. Sit back and relax."

To her surprise, she did just that, pillowing her head

on her hands. A breeze whispered over her, cooling her, inviting her to relax.

"What's got you worried?" he asked after long minutes had passed.

It was tempting to tell him of the headaches of trying to revitalize the ranch, to give in to the worry and fatigue of the last year. If she did, though, she feared she'd find it too comforting.

She'd already told him far more about her past than most people knew. It didn't seem fair to burden him with the problems of the present as well.

Before she could give in to the need to confide in him any further, she shook off her drowsiness and pushed herself up. "Time to get back to work."

For a minute, she thought he was going to argue, but then he nodded.

The trip had to be made. He'd put it off as long as possible. He told Johanna he needed a day off. She hadn't asked for an explanation, for which he was grateful.

"You took your time coming," Wingate said. As he had on previous occasions, he'd kept Cade waiting in the library for close to an hour before making an appearance.

"I waited until I had something to report."

The general's eyes gleamed with interest. "What's she like?"

Cade took his time. "She's hardworking, talented, ambitious."

His boss fixed on to the last. "Ambitious, you say?"

"She wants to make a success of her ranch," Cade said cautiously, wondering where Wingate was heading.

"Loans? Outstanding debts?"

"The bank holds the note on the Double J. Her father took it out before he died last year."

"What's her present situation?"

"She'd like to buy more land, hire more men," Cade said reluctantly.

"So she needs money." A satisfied note entered Wingate's voice. "Good."

"Why all the questions?"

"Nothing you have to worry about. Keep watching her. See what makes her tick."

"That's all?"

"For now." The general scrubbed a hand through his iron-gray hair. "You have a problem with that?"

"I'd like to know where this is heading."

"You've been told what you need to know."

"What if I refuse?" Cade persisted.

"Did I tell you I've talked with an old friend of mine in the War Department? Just a friendly chat. He served under McClellan, just like your yellow-bellied brother did. Maybe they even knew each other."

Cade resisted the urge to ram his fist in Wingate's face for the remark about Noah. Very deliberately, he took a step back. Another. His hands clenched in fists at his sides, he took a tempering breath.

He focused on the growing tautness in his shoulders, the building ringing in his ears.

Breathe deep. Release.

Breathe deep. Release.

He worked now on unbending his fingers, one by one, forcing his shoulders to relax. He felt disgusted. With Wingate. With himself. "I'll let you know when I've learned more."

Loyalty exacted a heavy price, Cade reflected as he made the journey back to the Double J. A very heavy price. In a matter of minutes, Wingate had succeeded in reminding him of how he could destroy Noah with only a few words to the right person.

Cade scowled at the direction of his thoughts. How much of himself could he sacrifice in an effort to safeguard his brother? More important, how could he live with himself after betraying Johanna?

A self-loathing such as he'd never known chilled him. He had done Wingate's bidding before. None of those things had mattered; they were simply a matter of straightening out trouble in Wingate's various holdings. Never before had he been forced to involve himself with someone whom he could, and probably would, hurt.

*Stop brooding*, he ordered himself. *You did what you had to.*

Somehow, though, it didn't make him feel any better.

## *Chapter Four*

Cade, isn't it about time you told me the truth?" Johanna asked as they worked on cleaning tack and saddles. After her revelations, she wanted—no, she needed—to know more of the man who had come to mean so much to her in such a short time.

He stood motionless, his hand still on the bridle he was cleaning. "The truth?"

"About why you're here."

"I'm here to work."

She looked at him in exasperation. "You're not an ordinary ranch hand. Even if you're better with horses than anyone I know, outside of my dad and George, you don't have the look."

"What do I look like?"

"Oh, maybe one of those Brinks detectives I read about in the *Gazette*." She entered into the guessing game with spirit, giving her imagination free rein.

Her words hit too close to home. "Nothing so glamorous, I'm afraid. I'm just a cowpoke." His lips quirked into a wry smile. "Right now, a cowpoke with a job. And I've got the prettiest boss any man could hope for." He cupped her chin in his hand. "For the first time in a long time, I like what I'm doing." That, at least, was the truth.

"I'm glad," she said simply.

He'd almost given himself away with his fumbling words. The truth, the whole truth, was bound to come out. The only question was when.

Truth and honesty. Words he'd lived by. And now they were his enemy.

Apparently Johanna sensed his discomfort with the subject, for she let it drop. They picked up their work, quickly reestablishing the easy rhythm between them. Only later did she remember that he hadn't answered her question.

Cade wiped his eyes, which were gritty with fatigue. Sleep had been a long time coming last night. Johanna's question had rattled him more than he cared to admit. Whatever his inner turmoil, though, he couldn't let it interfere with his work.

Measuring a length of pine two-by-four, he thought of what he was creating here. A home.

*Home.*

It had been a long time since he'd used the word. Even longer since he'd had one. He still didn't. Unless you counted the ranch north of Denver.

Johanna was making him want something he'd forgotten the meaning of. The realization made him angry. He didn't need to be reminded of what might have been.

Grimly, he finished sawing the lengths of wood. Gradually his anger slipped away, replaced by determination. He needed to help her finish the barn. The Double J needed the extra stalls if it were to grow. Even more, he needed to do this for Johanna.

Without talking, Johanna held a length of wood. They worked quietly with a coordination that should have gratified him. Instead it emphasized what he was risking with his dishonesty.

"Cade, what's bothering you?"

Johanna's voice startled him, but no more than her words. He'd thought he'd kept his worry to himself. Obviously he wasn't as successful as he'd hoped. "What makes you think something's bothering me?" He kept his voice light.

"These," she said, tracing the lines around his mouth.

Gently, but deliberately, he eased away from her touch. "Hey, are we going to stand around talking or get this thing finished?"

He sensed her reluctance to drop the subject as she held one end. He was especially proud of that piece of woodwork.

"I wish you felt you could trust me."

He almost blurted it out. *It's not you I don't trust. It's me.*

"I do trust you," he said quietly. "But some things aren't mine to share."

"I know you had a life before you came here. This thing you can't tell me . . . is it related to that?"

In this, at least, he could be honest. "Yes."

"Thank you."

"For what?"

"For not lying to me."

A wave of guilt washed over him at her words. "Johanna . . ."

"Yes?"

He wanted to ask for her forgiveness, but to do so would require telling her everything. And that, he was not prepared to do.

Not yet.

The rhythm of measuring, sawing, and nailing soothed his nerves, and he managed to push away his worry. For now. For now it was enough that he was with Johanna. He caught himself pausing every once in a while just to watch her. He didn't believe he'd ever grow tired of looking at her.

She always managed to look lovely, yet she paid little attention to her appearance. Her lack of vanity was one of the many facets of her personality that fascinated him. Right now, her lower lip was caught between her teeth.

"Something wrong?" he asked.

She looked up. "Nothing that can't be fixed." She paused. "Did I button my shirt the wrong way?"

"What? Uh . . . no."

"Why are you staring?"

"Because you're beautiful." So beautiful that she gave his heart a warm pulse.

He blew the hair from her eyes, brushing a wisp of a kiss against her forehead.

A soft laugh escaped her. "I've got saw sawdust in my hair, dirt under my fingernails, and manure on my boots."

He took her hands and brought them to her sides. "You have fire in your hair, hands that show you know how to work, and the most kissable lips I've ever seen."

The denial hovering on her lips died at his last words. "Most kissable lips?"

"Definitely." He touched his lips to hers to prove his point.

"You're being kind."

"Does this feel kind?" he asked, kissing her once more.

A slow flush crept into her cheeks. She gave him a quick smile before ducking her head, her hair curtaining her face.

Cade considered her shyness a pleasant contrast to most of the women he had known. They were skilled in the art of flirtation and accepted compliments as their due, while Johanna seemed inordinately pleased with each one. His hands tightened around the hammer he was holding as he remembered that he had no right to give her compliments when he couldn't give her the most important thing of all—the truth.

Soon, he promised himself, he'd find a way to end the lies between them. Then he'd be free to give her everything she needed. Until then . . .

"Cade?"

"Hmm?"

"You were staring again."

"Sorry. I was thinking."

"You looked so troubled. Won't you let me help you?" She hesitated. "Is it money? If it is, maybe I could—"

"It's not money," he said, more harshly than he'd intended. Her quick generosity, given her circumstances, stunned and shamed him.

Her eyes clouded. "I didn't mean to offend you."

"You didn't. I just wasn't expecting . . . I know you're struggling."

"If you're trying to say money's tight right now, you're right. But I could part with a few dollars if it would help."

"No one's ever done anything like that for me," he said, his voice husky. "But I don't need money." He needed something much more precious. He needed her forgiveness, but he couldn't tell her that. Not now. Not yet.

She gave him an uncertain look. "I know I'm not paying you what you could earn somewhere else. A man with your experience."

"You're paying me plenty. Now let's get back to work. Okay?"

"Okay."

He was careful to keep his worries to himself for the rest of the day. Johanna didn't need any more on her plate than she already had. He only wished his problem could be solved with money.

Her warm heart would—should—compel a man, a better man, to keep his distance. It should, but it didn't. It drew him even as he told himself he should stay away.

She deserved better than a man who could only offer her lies.

If this were any other job, and Johanna were any other woman, he would have already resigned and handed the assignment over to another of Wingate's men. Permanently. Never before had he allowed himself to become personally involved in a job, and Cade knew he was violating his own code of honor.

He couldn't leave Johanna alone to face the general. He didn't doubt her strength. This was a woman who faced life square in the eye, and seldom did anyone underestimate her a second time. She lived in a harsh, unforgiving climate that demanded hard work every day of the year. But there was an innocence to her that was no match for Wingate's brand of ruthlessness.

When quitting time came, he kept working.

"You looking for a raise?" George asked. The words were light, but his tone was not.

The foreman had taken to stopping by the corral. He'd said it was to watch, but Cade knew differently. George didn't trust him. A humorless smile touched Cade's lips as he conceded that the foreman had every right not to trust him.

Cade continued his work with the gelding. Someday he'd make a fine cutting horse. "Nope."

"You don't talk much, do you?" George observed.

"I always figured I learned more listening than talking."

The foreman gave him a shrewd look. "And keep yourself private from others."

Cade hunched a shoulder in acknowledgment. "There's that."

"Johanna's got a lot riding on this season."

"I know."

"You're pretty good," George allowed, the grudging note of admiration in his voice causing a smile to tug at Cade's lips.

The smile wasn't returned.

With a shrug, Cade turned back to his work. "I'm doing my job. Got a problem with that?"

"No," the foreman said slowly. "No problem. Just stick

to your work and we'll get along fine." Still, he didn't leave. "She cares about you."

Cade had no answer for that.

"Don't hurt her."

"I don't plan on it."

George gave him a long look. "I think you mean that. That don't mean she won't get hurt. I've known Johanna since she was a baby. She doesn't give her heart easily. In fact, she's never even—"

Whatever he'd been about to say ended abruptly. It wasn't hard to figure out what he'd left unsaid, though. Johanna was as innocent as a baby. George was right to be concerned about her.

"Forget I said anything," he said gruffly. "She wouldn't take kindly to my interfering." The sober expression on George's long face made it appear even longer.

"No," Cade said evenly. "I don't suppose she would."

"And I wouldn't take kindly to anybody hurting her." George leveled a steady gaze at Cade. The threat behind the words was left unspoken.

*Message received,* Cade telegraphed back. When George left, Cade let out a pent-up breath. He felt like he'd been hanging over a precipice. Under other circumstances, he had a feeling he'd like the foreman. Heck, he *did* like him. He figured he and George might have been friends if Johanna wasn't standing between them.

After letting the horse cool down, Cade led the big gelding back to the barn.

He pulled off his shirt, which had been plastered to his back. A slight breeze found its way through the high windows of the barn. He let the cool air trickle over him.

He started measuring lengths of board, thinking of

the promise he'd made to Johanna that they'd finish framing the new barn before cold weather set in.

Late afternoon stretched into evening, evening into night.

Looking tired and disheveled, Johanna walked in. "I wanted to talk to you earlier but had to see to some broken fences. I saw George talking with you. Anything I should know about?"

"He was just giving me some advice."

"Warning you off me?"

He hesitated before nodding briefly. "You could say that."

"He has no right," she began.

"He cares about you." George had made his feelings plain. He wouldn't take kindly to anyone hurting Johanna. Cade respected that.

"You're right. Still, he shouldn't—"

"Leave it. No harm done."

She looked at him uncertainly. "You're sure?"

"Yeah. George is a good man. He's just looking out for you. You're lucky to have him as a friend."

"I know. He can't seem to get it through his head that I'm grown up." The last was said with more affection than exasperation. "Now that we've established that I'm all grown up, why don't you tell me what you're doing here?"

"Just trying to keep my promise," he said, his voice warming her, the substance of him in it, strong, steady, full of honor and integrity.

She didn't ask what promise. She already knew. The promise he'd given her that they'd finish framing the barn.

She didn't argue with him this time over the rightness of his unpaid work, but placed a hand on his arm. "Thank you." Her glance rested briefly on the scars that bisected his chest.

He no longer felt self-conscious, as he had when she'd first seen the scars, but he still felt exposed and started to shrug on his shirt.

She laid a hand on his, stilling it. "Don't. They don't bother me."

"No?"

Soft color shaded her cheeks as she admitted that the scars did bother her, but not in the way he meant. "Only because they mean you were hurt." Deliberately, she pressed a kiss to his shoulder.

The touch of her lips acted as balm to a pain long buried. The warmth of her breath on his neck stretched his nerves taut. His gaze collided with hers, and his heart pounded against his chest at what he read in her eyes.

Wisps of hair escaped the clips to curl in damp tendrils along Johanna's temples. Cade's fingers itched to brush them back from her face. With an effort, he kept his hands at his sides.

Her hands traced the path her lips had forged just moments earlier.

Her understanding should have warmed him. Instead, it filled him with self-revulsion.

Johanna made him feel things he hadn't felt in years. Things he thought long dead. Things he believed he'd buried in a battlefield more than a dozen years ago.

She'd reached out to him and found what Cade hadn't even known about himself. She was teaching him to care—to care about others, but mostly about himself.

How long had it been since he honestly cared what happened to him?

Too long.

His thoughts swirled together, leading him to center a swift kiss upon her lips. That, at least, was honest. His feelings for her were real.

Johanna moved her fingers over her lips, and he longed to kiss them again.

He'd acted as Wingate's right-hand man for so long that he'd forgotten how to be anything else. Well, all that was going to change. *Had* changed, he corrected.

Cade had his own code of ethics. He'd developed it over the years, a hard-won set of rules he lived by. If they didn't match those of others, they at least allowed him to keep his self-respect.

And that was his biggest fear. He was in danger of losing that respect. If he lost that, he'd have nothing to offer her.

Or himself.

# *Chapter Five*

"What do you say we take off for a couple of hours?" Cade suggested on Sunday following church services. "Pack a picnic and go for a buggy ride."

She made a face. "I've got fences to mend."

"They can wait. I'd say we've earned a little rest."

Suddenly she smiled. "I'd say you're right. I'll ask Sarah if she'll take care of the food."

Half an hour later, Cade rapped on her door. "Ready?"

At her nod, he gestured to the buckboard. "Your chariot awaits."

He drove quickly, competently, as he did everything, she thought. When he pulled the buggy under a grove of aspens, she gave a tiny sigh of pleasure.

"How did you know this was my favorite place?"

"You've been here before?"

"Pa used to bring me here after we'd finished up for the day."

"If you'd rather, we can go somewhere else."

"Not on my account."

He tossed her a blanket and carried a bulging sack to a level patch of ground. With a flourish, he pulled out two yellow apples and thick sandwiches wrapped in a white cloth.

He watched as Johanna ate two sandwiches and an apple. He dabbed at her mouth with a cloth napkin, the casual gesture oddly intimate.

The happiness in her eyes touched him in an unfathomable way, and he knew he wanted to keep that look in her eyes forever.

He couldn't keep from touching her hair, letting his fingers sift through it. It spilled over his hand, a living thing of gold and red that caught and held the afternoon sun. Fascinated, he watched as the colors shifted—first lightening, then darkening, as the fading light played over it.

"You have beautiful hair," he said, unable to free it from his grasp.

"I always wanted to have dark hair," she said, a slight frown knitting her brows.

He couldn't imagine anything more lovely than the fall of amber silk splashing over his hand. "Why?"

"I wanted to be like my ma. Her hair was the color of the sky at midnight. If mine had been darker, I could have pretended she was my real ma."

He heard the lingering pain of a little girl wanting to belong to someone. He saw memories and more in her eyes. He saw love and loss, and a heart-wrenching sadness.

"Hey," she said, apparently sensing his feelings. "It's all right. My parents said they loved me just as I was." A soft smile touched her lips. "Red hair and freckles."

Cade would never describe her hair as simply red. The infinite shades, ranging from gold to russet, denied such a simple description. He traced the dusting of freckles on her nose. "I do, too."

He watched as color suffused her face. She had no idea how beautiful she was. In her, he caught a glimpse of how Trudy must have looked twenty years ago, before the disease had ravaged her body.

Thoughts of Trudy were too close to his reason for being here. Deliberately, he forced them away. There'd be time enough to deal with them later.

He picked up the corners of the cloth and tied them into a loose knot. He stashed the whole thing in the back of the buckboard. "Dishes are done."

"We'd better get back."

"Not yet. Tell me what puts that faraway look in your eyes sometimes."

"You don't miss much, do you?"

He shrugged. "Not much."

A quick laugh betrayed her nervousness.

"Hey," he said, taking her hand and squeezing it lightly. "You don't have to if it makes you that uncomfortable."

"It's not that."

"Then what?"

She was tempted to overlook the question and switch to a safer subject, but the sincerity and interest she read in his eyes invited confession.

Maybe talking about it would help. A deep breath steadied her. "Sometimes I played the 'what-if' game."

"The what?"

"What if my mother . . . my other mother . . . had

wanted me and hadn't given me up? What would my life have been like? What would I have been like?"

"That can be a dangerous game."

"You're right. But I couldn't help wondering if I had done something differently, if I had been different, then maybe . . ."

"Don't," he ordered. "You're not to blame for any of it. It. Was. Not. Your. Fault." He said each word slowly for emphasis.

"My mind knows that. But sometimes my heart doesn't. I used to lie awake at night, wondering why she didn't want me."

He reached for her at the same moment she cried, "Why? Why didn't she want me enough to keep me?"

"Johanna," he began softly, watching as first anguish and then embarrassment crossed her face. "Let it go, honey. Don't fight it anymore."

"I'm not—" She clutched his shirt as the sobs overtook her.

He stroked her back and waited for the storm to pass. When the sobs subsided into an occasional hiccup, he eased her away enough that he could look at her.

"I know it hurts. But you can't keep blaming yourself for something that wasn't your fault. You were a baby. You had no say in what other people did."

"I kept thinking there must be something wrong with me. Otherwise my mother would have kept me."

"Have you ever thought that maybe your mother gave you up because she wanted something better for you, something she couldn't give you?"

She'd never thought of it that way. Chewing her lip, she wondered if he could be right.

"You sound like you know what she was feeling."

He was treading on dangerous ground here and picked his words carefully. "It's not hard to imagine. A young, probably unwed woman, looking to give her child a better life. It happens."

"I know."

The pain that crept into her voice tore at his insides, and he longed to erase it from her life as though it had never happened. Yet then, he acknowledged, she wouldn't be the woman she was.

He yearned to wipe away the self-doubt he read in her eyes and then wondered at his reaction to her. More than a decade had passed since he'd worried about anyone else other than his brother.

"You're right. I can't change the past. No one can."

Her shoulders straightened, and he sensed the fighting spirit beneath the fragile air. More than anything, he admired such strength.

"I just wish I could convince you to believe in yourself, to realize you're a beautiful woman, one who has more love to give than most of us ever dream of having."

"I want to," she said. "But I'm afraid of depending on you, of caring about you."

"You don't have to be afraid with me. I'll never leave you." Gently, oh, so gently, Cade traced the delicate line of her jaw with his lips. They glided, stroked, and excited with their feather-light touch. When he lowered his mouth to find her own, she responded instinctively, opening her lips to his.

The sweetness he found inside was so incredible, it threatened to take his breath away. Never had he tasted such nectar.

She wound her arms about his neck.

His mouth dipped lower to find the vulnerable hollow of her throat.

Johanna felt his hands tremble as they held her. This strong man was trembling—and she had caused it. The knowledge filled her with wonder.

His kiss feathered across her brow, a caress as gentle as a summer breeze. His lips traced the curve of her cheek, to pause at the lobe of her ear, and, finally, to rest upon her own.

Her mouth opened to receive his as a flower lifts its head to the sun, seeking its warmth.

"We have all the time in the world." His words triggered the unwanted knowledge that he still faced his greatest hurdle—that of telling Johanna the truth.

"All the time in the world," she repeated, her eyes shining with the promise of tomorrows filled with newfound joy.

The happiness reflected in her eyes was a double-edged sword. He had put that there; he could just as easily destroy it when she learned of his deceit. He was locked into a web of lies that seemed bent on keeping them apart.

She slipped her hands beneath his shirt to finger the scars. "Can you tell me about it?"

He shook his head. "Not now, honey. Like I said, it was a long time ago. I don't want to dredge up the past. Especially when I can't change it."

"Yet you want me to tell you about my past," she reminded him. "It works both ways."

He gave her a crooked grin. "I guess you're right." He looked at her keenly. "Are you sure you want to hear this? It's not very pretty."

She touched his cheek. "I'm sure."

"I was seventeen when I enlisted," he began. "Green and eager to do my part." His laugh was brittle. A fine sheen of perspiration broke out across his forehead.

Something in his voice changed. It was almost imperceptible, but Johanna heard it. He was confiding things he didn't usually share with others. Or maybe she just wished he were.

"What happened?" Her gaze was too penetrating.

He focused on his breathing, working for slow, steady breaths that wouldn't betray what the memories did to him. Still, after all these years.

"War happened. Death happened. Too much. After a while, you learn that there is no black or white, only a million shades of gray that kept getting grayer by the year. I don't think I even knew what was right or wrong after a while. I just kept going, trying to make sense in a world that had lost all reason. In the end, I think I had stopped caring about right and wrong. I just wanted to survive."

Cade revealed only what he chose to reveal about his life, she thought. In the past minutes, he'd been surprisingly open.

He had admitted to weakness. That very admission seemed a strength, at least to her eyes. It took an exceptional man to own up to faults, with no excuses, no justifications for what he saw as failure.

She knew, without being told, that he had never stopped caring about right and wrong. There was a quiet stillness to him, a deep and abiding belief in truth and justice that he backed up with both courage and honor.

She heard that, but it was the utter defeat in his tone

that moved her most. Johanna willed the tears, still clinging to her lashes, not to fall. Cade didn't want her sympathy. He'd be uncomfortable and embarrassed if he ever got a glimpse of it.

Being around Cade had a way of bringing her emotions to the surface, even the ones she wanted to hold at bay. She was normally more reserved around men, always believing she was destined for quiet relationships. She averted her face, knowing her feelings were reflected in her eyes.

He caught the slight movement. With gentle fingers, he captured her chin and forced her to face him.

She attempted to brush the wetness away from her lashes, but he stilled her hand.

"Don't." He raised his hand and, with his knuckles, skimmed away the glistening moisture that had spilled over onto her cheeks.

"I'm not crying."

"I can see that." The gentle humor in his voice nudged a smile from her.

"I'm not," she insisted.

He brought his hand to his lips and tasted the salt of her tears.

She watched him and sucked in her breath at the oddly intimate gesture.

"It's all right to cry. Don't be ashamed of your tears. They're honest." He looked at her curiously. "Are they for me?"

Miserably, she nodded.

"No one's ever cried for me before." His voice turned husky. "I never wanted them to." He paused. "Until now."

She looked up, not sure she'd heard correctly. "You're not angry?"

"With you? Never."

The sincerity in his voice convinced her he meant what he said. A sweet warmth stole through her as the significance of that dawned on her. A week ago, even a few days ago, he'd have withdrawn into himself if she'd breached the invisible boundaries that had so far defined their relationship. Now, he accepted her tears and the caring that had prompted them.

She took his hand in hers, wanting to erase the loneliness that had been his sole companion for too many years. Tears now streamed down her cheeks unchecked.

She looked down at their linked hands. Her hand was not delicate—it was more capable than pretty—but right now, at this moment, it felt fragile and feminine in his grasp.

"It's over now. I survived. Even when I didn't want to. I must have been born under a lucky star."

She pressed his hand to her lips, wanting to absorb his pain and knowing she couldn't. "Tell me the rest."

"You're sure you want to hear?"

"Yes."

He kissed her before continuing. "From then on, I didn't much care what happened. It made me take risks no sane man would." A shutter dropped over his eyes as scene after scene unfolded in his mind. Unconsciously, he rubbed his left side, where a bullet had once embedded itself. He had dug it out with his own knife, after sterilizing it over an open fire.

After long moments, he looked up at Johanna. She had remained silent during his recital, but her eyes held something brighter than pity, more moving than simple compassion.

"I was promoted. The war ended." He gave a short laugh.

"What did you do?" she whispered.

"I went west and met"—he paused—"someone from my old outfit. He offered me a job."

"And your family?"

"My parents died a long time ago." Again, the faraway look entered his eyes. "It's been just me and my brother for a while now."

"You're close?"

"Yeah. You could say that." He coughed to cover the huskiness that had crept into his voice. "Noah's five years older than me. He sort of looked out for me when we were growing up.

"When our parents died, there wasn't any money. Noah enlisted, and he left me with our aunt. He wasn't a fighter, hated the thought of bloodshed, but he wanted to do his part. Plus we needed the money. He sent his pay to Aunt Sally to help out. She had five kids of her own."

Was that wistfulness she heard in his voice? She wasn't imagining it. Cade Larrabee, ex-soldier and wrangler, loved his brother deeply.

She tried to read between the lines. "What's he like?"

Pride and love lit his eyes from the inside out. "Noah's an idealist. A hero. Not like me."

She let that pass. "Where is he now?"

"I bought a place near Denver. Hired a husband and wife to look after him."

"You love him very much."

"Yes," he said quietly, a touching admission from

this big, strong man. "I wonder if he hadn't had me to take care of, he might not have joined up, might not have come home without his legs."

"Guilt," she said softly.

He didn't answer that. "What do you say we leave all this stuff where it belongs, in the past? We have a whole future in front of us."

She felt something move in her chest. Hope. But layering that was fear.

Could their love override the scars of the past? Could she erase the loneliness that was so much a part of him and make him believe in a forever kind of love, the kind her parents had shared for more than thirty-five years? She was honest enough to admit that nothing less would do for her.

She could admit to herself now that she loved him. If only she could believe she could have him. If only he loved her in return.

Whatever time they had, she would treasure. *It would be enough. It had to be.*

She trusted him, she realized with a start. He had worked his way into her life, into her heart. She'd been in love with him for a couple of weeks, but the trust—that was new.

It was an odd feeling, this trust in someone outside her circle. As if something had been returned to her before she'd even noticed it was missing.

On Saturday, she'd hoped they might have a repeat of the picnic they'd shared six days before. When she saw Cade with his saddlebags, she knew her hope wasn't to be realized.

She'd known a man like Cade wouldn't stick around a small-time outfit like the Double J forever. With what she prayed was a normal smile, she asked, "Going somewhere?"

"I've got to go to Denver for a couple of days. Don't worry. I'll be here bright and early Monday morning."

"I wasn't . . ." The lie died on her lips. "I'm glad you're coming back," she said instead.

He brushed his lips over hers. "Johanna, I think you know how I feel. I want—"

She put a finger to his lips. "Don't," she whispered. "I'm not ready. We're not ready. Not yet."

She needed time to adjust to the things she was discovering about herself and about him. She wanted what her parents had enjoyed. Someone with whom to share the ups and downs of life. Someone to rejoice with her and to cry with her. Someone who would make her feel loved and cherished. Someone she could count on.

Until he'd found his way into her life, she'd been content. Not happy, perhaps, but content. And that was the way she'd wanted it.

Wasn't it?

The question taunted her with unrelenting persistence, demanding she give it attention. The question, and it was a big one, was: If she let him into her life, what then? What became of her carefully ordered existence? Did she dare take that chance? Did she dare not?

Was it a good feeling, being the other half of a couple? Or did you have to give up part of yourself to unite with another? Was it worth the risk? Once, she'd thought she knew. Now she wasn't sure.

Would it be the same if he kissed her again? Would

she feel that same quiet intensity when he touched his lips to hers? Softly demanding. Sweetly inviting. Would he kiss her again? More important, did she want him to?

That question gave way to others.

What would it be like to know you could stretch out your hand and someone else would take it in his own? She looked at her hand, remembering the way it had fit inside Cade's. His hand had been hard, like the man himself. But there would be gentleness too. It was that dichotomy that intrigued her. Strength tempered by gentleness.

He wasn't an easy man to know. Instinctively, she knew he wouldn't make a relationship easy, either. He would be demanding, sometimes asking more than she could give and other times giving more than she ever dreamed. Risky, that's what he was. And a woman foolish enough to get involved with him would risk her heart.

For a fraction of a heartbeat, she reflected on what it would be like to be cherished, really cherished. Would his kisses always stir her as his last one had? Or would she grow tired of them, tired of him, as the initial thrill faded and familiarity set in?

No!

That the answer came without hesitation disturbed her. Even more disturbing was that she was thinking about him at all. Thoughts of him invaded her working hours as well as her dreams.

Her life was fine just the way it was. She didn't need Cade Larrabee or his particular brand of charm. That's all it was, she assured herself. A good-looking face and a way with words. Well, they wouldn't work with her.

Satisfied that she had successfully managed to set

her priorities straight, she went back to work. The Double J demanded her full attention. She assured herself that was what she wanted. She didn't have time for a relationship—or anything else—with Cade. That settled, she felt better.

She folded up her thoughts and headed back to the barn.

## *Chapter Six*

Cade shielded his eyes against the glare of the late-afternoon sun that silhouetted the crests of the foothills with fiery crimson.

The Wingate mansion had never bothered him before, but now it loomed against the backdrop of mountain and sky, its stone turrets dwarfed by the stately pines surrounding it.

An unseasonable heat mingled with his own tense state to dampen his clothes with sweat. Impatiently, he tugged the string tie free and undid the top button of his shirt.

He didn't look forward to the upcoming meeting. He'd worked for Victor Wingate for over a decade, and for the most part, they'd been good years. Now he was leaving. His sense of honor demanded he confront the general in person to tell him he was resigning—and why.

He hadn't telegrammed. Surprise served well when approaching the enemy. *Military tactics die hard,* he thought wryly.

After being announced and kept waiting for thirty minutes, Cade acknowledged that he'd been outmaneuvered. When Victor Wingate marched into the room, Cade stood.

Old habits.

"My aide said you wanted to see me," Wingate said. Even with his once ramrod-straight back slightly stooped, he was still every inch the general. Every inch the man who had led his men into battle and conquered the enemy. Every inch the man Cade had respected for more than a dozen years.

Now he would end that relationship. Unfortunately, the respect had already vanished.

Cade watched as Wingate lowered his bulk into the leather chair behind the desk, folding his arms across his chest.

"Well, what do you want? I don't have all day." His mouth thinned to an uncompromising slit, Wingate tapped a pipe against the edge of the desk, glaring at the younger man.

"You never wanted Trudy to find her daughter, did you?" The question wasn't one he'd planned to ask. He'd intended to resign and then leave.

Wingate templed his fingers, his elbows resting on his chest. "No."

Even though he'd expected it, Wingate's answer still shocked Cade. "Then why go to all the trouble to have me find Johanna?"

"I like to know who I'm dealing with."

That rang true. Wingate had earned his reputation the hard way: on the battlefield, in the mines, in the boardrooms of banks. Part of his reputation came by his insistence upon knowing the enemy. The tactic had earned him numerous victories.

"What are you going to tell Trudy?"

"I'll tell her that we looked for her daughter but couldn't find any trace of her."

"Maybe I'll tell her."

"Go ahead." Wingate lit a cigar. "If you want to see her hurt."

"How could finding her daughter hurt her?"

"Trudy isn't strong. She doesn't need some poor relation coming around begging for a handout."

Cade bit back the angry words hovering on his tongue. "Johanna Kellerman's no beggar."

"She's got a bank note to pay off, right?" Wingate didn't give Cade a chance to answer. "Everyone's out for themselves. Once she finds out her mother's got money, she'll come sniffing around fast enough."

"You're going to bribe her to stay away from Trudy? Why tell her anything at all? Why not leave her alone?"

"Sooner or later, she's going to start looking for her mother." Wingate shrugged. "I'm just buying some insurance."

"Insurance?"

"To make sure she doesn't go looking. If I pay her off, I'll have leverage if she tries to cross me and contact Trudy."

Cade's lips tightened at the notion that Johanna could be bought. "What about Trudy?"

"If I tell Trudy we tried and didn't find anything, she'll give up."

"You're so sure about that?"

Wingate looked annoyed. "Trudy's my sister. She'll do what I say."

"She could surprise you this time."

"I think I know what's best for my sister."

Cade heard the warning and backed off. For now. He had no intention, though, of keeping Trudy from the daughter she'd waited twenty-seven years to see.

"You're wrong if you think you can buy Johanna off."

"Enough money buys everything. And everyone."

Wingate's answer to any of life's problems. Money.

"What are you so afraid of?" Cade asked.

The general drew himself up. Color came and went in his face. "You just keep an eye on her. Let me know if her financial situation changes significantly. I'll take care of the rest."

"You're wrong about Johanna." Cade couldn't help himself. He had to defend Johanna. He owed her that much.

Wingate grinned. "I never knew you to be sweet on any one woman. At least not for long. What's the matter? Getting soft?"

*What's the matter is working for you.* But Cade didn't say the words aloud. He knew Wingate was a tough-minded opponent, whether on the battlefield or off, but never before had he realized the extent of the man's ruthlessness. And greed.

Wingate was preparing to betray his own sister without so much as a thought to her feelings or her needs. All for money.

"I want out."

The general regarded Cade as though he were a puzzle to be solved. "Why?"

"I've been serving under you, then working for you, for over twelve years. It's time I got on with my life."

Wingate eyed Cade shrewdly. "You never complained before."

"Never had reason to." Cade lifted a shoulder. "Things change."

"You're thinking of finding a different job?"

"Maybe."

"You've lost sight of what's important."

"No. It's taken me a while, maybe too long, but I'm just beginning to find it."

Wingate inspected Cade with new interest. "Why don't you tell me about it?" When Cade hesitated, the general added, "We've been friends for a lot of years."

That's not how Cade would describe their relationship. "It's time I thought about settling down."

"Settling down? Have you got someone in mind?"

"I'm in love with Johanna." He was startled at hearing himself say the words aloud. He hadn't meant to blurt it out like that. Instinctively, he knew he'd made a tactical error. Still, he savored the taste of the words upon his lips, knowing they were the most important he would ever utter.

Wingate appeared unmoved. "So?"

"I can't continue working for you," Cade explained, watching the general warily. He knew Wingate wasn't feebleminded. Apparently, he was pretending to be dull-witted for reasons of his own.

"As soon as you've finished the job," Wingate said, "you're free to do whatever you want. If you want the woman, you're welcome to her. It's nothing to me either way. Though I'd hate to see you throw away your life on a little nobody like her."

Lightning bolts of anger flashed beneath Cade's skin. "That little nobody is your niece."

"A matter of chance. She'll never be a Wingate."

"Maybe she doesn't want to be."

The general snorted. "Look around you. Can you honestly tell me she wouldn't want a part of all this?"

Cade let his gaze wander around the opulent room, the carefully chosen furniture, the priceless rug, and wondered about Johanna's reaction. She'd undoubtedly appreciate their beauty, but the price of such things would never impress her.

"Yes."

"Then you're as stupid as my sister. She's willing to hand it all over, everything I've worked to build for her, to someone she hasn't set eyes on in twenty-seven years."

"What she wants to do with her own money is her choice."

"Trudy owns forty-nine percent of Wingate Enterprises. Do you think I'd let her give it away to some little upstart with no breeding, no family background?"

So that was it.

"I'm through," Cade said, stressing each syllable and ignoring the reference to Johanna.

The general didn't appear upset. He examined his fingernails. "I hate to lose you, Cade." A regretful look crossed his face. "I guess your loyalty is just so much lip service, isn't it?"

"Loyalty?"

"You told me you'd do anything to protect Noah, but now you're letting a woman come between you and your brother."

Cade gripped the desk in front of him. Wingate was a master of manipulation. He knew just when to apply the pressure, and when to back off.

Cade thought of Noah and how the general could destroy the fragile peace he'd managed to achieve. The next moment Johanna's face, her eyes shining with trust, flashed before his face. Whatever happened with Noah, they'd work it out together. He turned to leave.

Wingate's next words halted him. "I suppose you won't mind if I tell my niece you've been working for me."

Cade forced himself to keep his voice casual even as a chill sprinted down his spine. "What do you mean?" Deliberately, he kept his back to the general, wanting time to compose himself. He'd erred badly by giving away too much already.

"I think she's entitled to hear the truth. That you tracked her down, wormed your way into her confidence, and then betrayed her." Wingate's voice rang with self-righteousness and something more—triumph?

It wasn't the truth, but it was close enough. Acknowledging the inevitable, Cade turned slowly. "What do you want?" He thrust aside the urge to close his hands around the man's throat and met the general's gaze. Cold. Never had he seen such cold eyes. Why had he never noticed before the emptiness in Wingate's eyes?

"I want to make sure she never bothers my sister."

Cade remained impassive under Wingate's inspection, his emotions once more in check.

Cade regretted his earlier anger. It wouldn't help Johanna, and it had fired Wingate's temper. He watched as the older man's fist clenched and his nostrils flared.

"You don't want me for an enemy, Larrabee."

Cade recoiled from a cold so intense that it touched his very core. He stood. "You're sick. There's no way I'll let you get away with hurting Johanna."

"Don't start spouting your petty morality to me," Wingate said. "It's a little late for that, don't you think? You'll do whatever it takes to get the job done. Just like you've always done."

"What do you mean?"

"Exactly what I said. You've done my bidding in the past. So don't give me this malarkey about how you've changed. I don't buy it. And, if you're honest, you don't either. You know," Wingate said reflectively, "you and I are a lot alike. That's why we've gotten along so well over the years."

Nauseated at the possibility that Wingate was right, Cade stared at him. He shook his head as though to deny it.

"You don't want to believe it, do you?"

Something dark and uncontrollable threatened to explode within him, causing him to struggle to steady his breathing. "You're wrong about me."

Wingate snorted. "If I am, it's your loss. You start going soft, and you don't stand a chance in this world. You of all people ought to know that." He eyed his opponent slyly. "What about the Kellerman woman? What if I tell her you went there with the sole purpose of getting close to her?"

Cade took a menacing step forward.

"I can have five men here before you take another step," Wingate told him. "But you'd still like to strangle me, wouldn't you?"

Cade's growl was answer enough.

"Interesting," the general mused. "In all the years I've known you, I've never seen you lose your temper. Now, within the space of a few minutes, you lose it twice." When Cade remained silent, he continued, "We've always gotten along well. But now you've fallen under a woman's spell. You can't even think straight."

Wingate was right about one thing. Cade's feelings for Johanna weren't casual. He'd never before felt this strong sense of connection and rightness with any woman.

Not until Johanna.

With a visible effort, Cade checked his anger yet again. He would get nowhere this way. He swallowed hard in an effort to get hold of his temper. "Why would you tell Johanna I work for you?" he asked in what he hoped was a reasonable tone. "You'd be cutting off your only source of information to her."

"I won't have to tell her," Wingate said, "if you do as you're told." He smiled affably and patted Cade's shoulder. "Let's have no more talk like that. We've always had a good working relationship. I'd hate to see anything interfere with that."

Cade deliberately shrugged off Wingate's hand, not bothering to hide his distaste. He knew enough about his boss to know that Wingate wouldn't be dissuaded from his goal. His only hope was to pretend to stick with the job and find a way to help both Trudy and Johanna while protecting Noah at the same time.

"I'll do my job," he said at last and started to leave.

At the door, he paused. His gaze pinned Wingate's and held it. "Don't ever tell me again we're alike. You and I are nothing alike. Nothing."

He turned and walked away. This time he didn't look back.

Cade couldn't get away from the house and its owner fast enough. He felt as though he was suffocating. He rode quickly, stopping only when he came to a lookout point.

His gaze spanned the breathtaking vista before him, no less spectacular in the evening dusk. Greedily, he drank in great gulps of fresh air. He turned to face the wind, savoring the sharp, cleansing feeling of it.

Overhead, he beheld the lofty wingspan of an eagle riding the air in search of prey. In the distance, he could see a herd of elk grazing at the edge of a clearing.

It was getting dark now, twilight closing in around him, but it wasn't a friendly twilight. Despite the surrounding beauty of the area, this spot was not peaceful. Or maybe he was reacting to his meeting with Wingate.

He stretched as though to free himself of invisible manacles. For too long, he'd allowed habit to chain him to a man who used and then discarded people. Not that he'd been blind to the general's faults, but he'd accepted them as part of the man who had led his troops into battle.

Now his loyalty to such a man sickened him. He shuddered at the thought that, if he'd stayed, he might succumb to the forces that drove Wingate, losing his humanity and compassion in a quest for power.

He had lied to Wingate.

And he would do it again if he had to. He had told the general he'd do the job, but he would find a way to protect Johanna as well as Noah. She meant too much to him. She was life and breath to him. Without her, he would have no reason for being.

He had to buy time.

Every second, every minute with her was one more opportunity to forge the bonds between them. One more bit of armor against the pain to come.

If he'd learned anything about her in the past weeks, he'd learned that she valued honesty above all things. Integrity shone in everything she did.

Cade rode as though possessed, anxious to put as many miles between Wingate and himself as he was to return to Johanna.

In his mind, he replayed the conversation until each word was burned into his memory. Wingate was right about one thing: if Johanna learned from him how he, Cade, had insinuated himself into her life from someone else, she would hate him.

The only solution was for him to tell her the truth himself. He'd known it all along. Yet he desperately searched for some other way, even knowing as he did so that it was hopeless.

His gut tightened at the thought of what lay ahead and what he'd have to do. Despite his brave talk, he knew he had no choice. By protecting Noah, he'd have to betray Johanna. And by betraying her, he'd lose her, the woman who had come to mean more to him than life itself.

He'd never had much use for religion. His ma had done her best to teach him and Noah from the Good Book, but after she'd died, he hadn't so much as set a foot inside a church or opened a Bible.

Too many nights alone as a child, he supposed. Too many promises broken by his pa, until he learned somewhere way deep down that the only people he could depend upon were Noah and himself.

Now he wished he remembered some of the prayers his ma had tried to teach him. He longed to pray that he could make things right with Johanna, could convince her that he loved her, would always love her.

Maybe, just maybe, he could pray even if he didn't recall the right words. And so he did. When he uttered the last word, a sense of peace settled over him like a warm blanket in the middle of winter.

With Johanna, there could be no halfway measures. He was in love with her, not infatuated, though he almost wished it were so. He could have dealt with that.

Love had a different flavor; it couldn't be rushed, neither could it be greedy. Love demanded freedom to grow. Love was a seed that must be nourished, nurtured as it unfolded, cherished as it blossomed into full bloom. Love was forever.

And he was frightened. More frightened than he'd ever been in his life.

Dusk had long since fallen by the time he reached the Double J. The night air had a bite to it. His breath emerged in puffs of steam. He knocked lightly on her door. The need to see Johanna kept him on the step even when good manners dictated he leave.

Just when he would have turned away, a candle flickered.

"Cade?" a voice called out.

"Yes."

The door swung open. "I was hoping you'd make it back tonight."

Cade grinned as he slipped his arms around Johanna's waist. "Miss me?" He sketched tiny patterns down her spine, nearly wiping away rational thought.

"Yes." No games between them. What they had was too important.

"I like to hear you say it."

"I missed you," she said, her voice whisper-soft.

"That's all I needed."

"I feel like you've been away forever," she confessed as he kissed her.

"It seems like I have."

"That feels so good," she murmured as he held her close, her words muffled against his chest. "I don't want you to ever stop holding me."

"There's so much I want to share with you." He stopped to turn her face to his, cupping her chin in his hand. "Do you know what I'm saying?"

"I think so."

"You make me want things I haven't dared let myself think about in years. You make me hungry for something I didn't think existed anymore. You make me feel when I thought all feeling was dead. I can't imagine my life without you in it."

Johanna was startled. It was a long speech for a man not given to fancy words.

Tears puddled in the corners of her eyes as she held him close. In many ways, she'd had a rough life, yet it didn't compare with the barren existence that Cade had endured for so many years. She cried silently for the lonely man she cradled in her arms.

*I'm here for you*, she wanted to say. Instead, she curled her arms around him and held him tighter.

For a fragment of a moment, they stayed there, locked together, their breath mingling.

A feeling of peace settled over him. The self-disgust he felt for the lie he was living wasn't enough to move him out of her embrace.

He felt he could stay this way forever, with Johanna's arms wrapped around him. He needed this, now more than ever. Now that he'd discovered just how far he was willing to go to protect her.

Never had anything felt so good, so right, as this sweet communion of spirit he felt with Johanna. With every bit of willpower he possessed, he freed himself, and looked at the woman who'd turned his life upside down in a few short weeks.

*Tell her the truth,* his conscience prodded him. *Better coming from you than from Wingate.* Still, he hesitated. *Tell her,* the voice persisted. *Tell her who you are and why you came here. If you do it now, there's a chance she won't throw you out.*

*Sure,* the other, cowardly side of himself argued. *Tell her you came here to spy on her and then report back to the man who convinced her mother to give her up in the first place.*

"Johanna, I have—"

She skimmed a finger along his lips. "Not now. Don't say anything. It's enough that you're here." She reached up to frame his face in her hands. "I know there's something bothering you. I also know you'll tell me when the time is right. Until then . . ." A smile brushed her lips. "I can wait."

Her simple trust shamed him even as it humbled him. He didn't deserve it, or her. But he was going to change all that. With only a few words, he could wipe away the lies that stood between them. He could also shatter the very fragile bond linking them.

Maybe it was a good thing she'd stopped his confession.

It gave him what he needed most—time. Every second with her, every minute, gave him more time to strengthen the ties between them. More armor against the pain he knew would come. More hope that, when it was over, she might find it in her to forgive him.

"I never want to hurt you." He realized he'd spoken the words aloud.

"I know."

Her simple faith warmed him. She was so trusting, so honest, that she couldn't conceive of anyone being otherwise.

Silently, he prayed he could keep the promise he'd just made.

"I have something to tell you," she said.

"Confession time?"

"Sort of."

"It sounds serious."

"It is." She took a deep breath. "I'm afraid if you stay much longer I won't be able to let you go. And that's not fair to you. I don't think I could bear it if you leave."

"I'm not leaving," he promised. "Not unless you ask me to."

"That's not going to happen."

"I hope you're right."

His words prompted a frown. "I don't understand—"

"It's nothing," he said, tunneling his hand beneath her hair. "Nothing important."

She melted against him. "I'm glad you're back."

"You said that already."

"So I did. Must be because I missed you so much." She pulled his hand to her lips and softly kissed his palm.

He replaced his hand with his lips.

The kiss was a dream come true. Her eyes closed, she memorized this moment—the heat of his lips, the rasp of his beard against her cheek, the sounds of the night.

"I didn't know it could be this way," she said when he raised his head, awe in her voice.

Her simple admission filled him with wonder while at the same time humbling him. His heart trembled, and he felt something in his stomach that he hadn't experienced in a long time.

Shyly, she put her arms around his neck, bringing his face at a level with hers. She touched her lips to his. He reeled under her power though her touch was as light as thistledown.

She rained tiny kisses along his throat, each a sweet promise for the future. It was all he could do to not let himself respond more fully to her diffident advances.

His control, which he'd always prided himself on, was now threatened by a touch so soft it barely registered, yet so potent that it honed his senses to a fine pitch.

"Johanna," he whispered, "you make me feel things I shouldn't be feeling."

*I know*, she responded silently, feeling the sweet ache of love. For an instant, she allowed herself to indulge in a fantasy: she and Cade married with the promise of children to come. She'd always wanted a big family, a house full of children and laughter and love.

His heart spoke to hers; hers answered in return. Silently, he was telling her what she longed to hear. She rested against him, content to draw from his quiet strength.

His chin rested on her head. He fingered the curls framing her face and inhaled the fresh scent that clung to her hair.

"I can't keep on this way," he said, his voice hoarse with repressed longing. "I can't keep working for you and pretending I feel nothing when the other men are around."

She didn't say anything, but waited.

"I think you know how I feel. I want to be a part of your life."

She murmured an inarticulate sound.

"If I'm wrong, tell me. But I need to hear it from you."

"You're not wrong," she managed to say. "But I'm not ready—"

He stopped her. "I know that. I don't want to rush you. But I'm not a patient man. I need to know what you're feeling."

"I couldn't ask you, or any man, to share the note on the ranch."

"What if he wanted to?"

Tears stung her eyes at his words.

"I understand pride. But it doesn't belong between two people who . . ." He didn't finish the sentence, and for that she was grateful.

"I know you're afraid of caring, of loving." There, he'd said it. "Don't let the past come between us. It can't hurt you anymore. Not unless you allow it. Let it go."

"I don't know if I can." Her eyes begged him to understand. "I want to. More than you know, I want to."

He brushed the back of his hand against her cheek. "That's enough. All I wanted to know was that I wasn't imagining what was happening between us."

"You weren't."

"If you ever want me to go away, you'll have to tell me. Because nothing else could make me leave you."

Warm hands cupped her face as he searched for an answer there.

She put a tentative hand to his cheek, touched by his declaration but still afraid to trust her own feelings. "Cade, you . . . me . . . how can you know for sure?"

"Because it's as much a part of me as breathing. You're a part of me."

*Johanna.* Her name was a prayer, a plea, a promise. He gathered her to him, cradling her in his arms. Still, he couldn't get enough of her. He felt her heartbeat race, matching the cadence of his own.

"I don't mean to rush you. I need to know that what we feel for each other is real."

"It's real," she whispered. "More real than anything has ever been before, but I'm afraid. Everyone I've ever loved has left me."

"We'll work everything out. Together." *We have to,* he added silently.

Cade liked to think he had too much integrity to give promises he didn't believe he could keep. He'd promised to help her frame the barn before cold weather set in. Simple. All that required was hours of hard work and skill.

He'd also promised not to leave her unless she asked

him to. Again, simple. Nothing would tear him away from her unless she told him to leave.

He knew Johanna was wary of caring too deeply. *Everyone I've ever loved has left me,* she'd said.

It was up to him to convince her that love was a promise they could keep together.

He laughed. Then he sobered and held out his arms.

She walked into them and let her head rest against his shoulder. He smelled of soap and leather. He drew her closer until she could scarcely breathe. When she drew a long, shuddering breath, he released her.

"This could become a habit," he said.

His words had her cheeks heating with color.

He traced a gentle finger along her jaw. A faint tremor fluttered in her stomach.

She felt like they'd reached a new understanding. Holding out her hand, she expected him to take it in his. Instead, he brought it to his lips and pressed a gentle kiss in the center of her palm.

Before she had time to absorb the sensation, he abruptly released it.

"I apologize," he said. "I had no right to make promises. Not yet."

The last two words were uttered so quietly that she almost missed them. Something in his voice alerted her that everything was not all right. She took a step back so that she might study his face.

He looked tired, with more than a hint of strain around his eyes. She knew he was worried about something. She had a funny feeling it had to do with her, but for the life of her, she couldn't figure out what it was.

The tension in his eyes dimmed her joy in the moment.

She couldn't understand where the sudden worry had come from. One minute they were sharing feelings, and the next he had turned inside himself, effectively shutting her out.

Everything was going well between them, so why did he look at her with such worry?

## *Chapter Seven*

Though Sarah, George's wife, was not much older than Johanna's own twenty-seven years, she had taken on the role of mother hen after the death of Johanna's parents. "Thought you'd sneak out before you had your breakfast, didn't you?"

"No. That is—" Johanna broke off when Sarah shook her head.

"I recognize lovesick when I see it. Why don't you tell me?"

Johanna felt Sarah's probing gaze and almost wished her friend weren't so perceptive.

"It's that Larrabee fellow, isn't it?" Sarah asked.

Sarah's words hit her like a douse of cold water. In love with Cade? They'd known each other for only a few weeks. She admitted she found him attractive, that she had even come to care for him. But love . . . that was something else.

She pretended an interest in the gouges that scarred

the old kitchen table as she tried to ignore the quivery sensations that danced down her spine. "Cade's nice enough."

Sarah snorted. "There's been something between you two right from the start."

"Are you asking if I love him?" Johanna heard herself say the words as if from a distance.

"Do you?"

She took refuge in briskness. "Cade and I enjoy each other's company. That's all."

Sarah refrained from saying anything more, and Johanna was grateful for her friend's tact. It took all of her self-discipline to concentrate on her work for the rest of the day.

She'd lied to Sarah. She did love Cade. Her insides tightened at the admission.

Cade was fast becoming the most important thing in her life. The admission came more easily than she anticipated, even after that little talk she'd given herself earlier. That, more than anything, worried her.

She couldn't avoid him indefinitely. When she found him working with Thunder in the corral, she couldn't help but stop and admire his way with the ornery stallion.

"Looking good," she called out.

He turned and tipped his hat. "Thanks."

With Cade's attention temporarily diverted, Thunder raised his front hooves. Johanna held her breath as Cade calmed the stallion with little more than a word and a flick of his wrist.

George came to stand beside her. "He's good."

"Yeah."

"Maybe a little too good."

She turned to frown at him. "What do you mean?"

"Have you asked yourself why he came here? Seems a mite convenient."

"What are you saying?"

"Nothin'. I just have a feeling about that fellow that don't sit quite right."

George's words caused a ripple of uneasiness to move through her.

Common sense took over. Once the season was over, Cade would most likely move on. She had known that all along. Cade would leave. That was the reason she was trying not to become too attached to him. There was only one problem. As reluctant she was to admit it, she wanted to grab hold of him and never let go.

Cade kept his voice low as he worked with Thunder. He liked working with the horses, especially the ill-tempered stallion. The horse had a mean streak, but his proud bearing tugged at Cade.

More, though, than the satisfaction of working with a truly fine animal was Johanna and the happiness he saw in her eyes. He'd do anything to keep it there.

Other events seemed to be spiraling out of his power, but work was something he could control.

He looked at her down-bent head, her hair catching the light and turning to gold. As if aware of his scrutiny, she raised her head just then, her eyes meeting his, her lips curved softly into a smile.

Yes, he'd do anything to make her happy. Anything but tell her the truth. Suddenly, the arguments he'd used last night to justify his delay fell flat. Time wouldn't change the fact that he'd lied to her.

Nothing could change that.

He stole another glance at her. He couldn't tell her. Not now. Not when her eyes were filled with happiness. Not when they regarded him with such trust. Not when all he wanted to do was take her into his arms and promise to love her forever.

*Coward.*

Johanna lifted a sack. "It's almost noon."

"Sounds good."

They ate their sandwiches with only the barest conversation between them.

She lifted her lips. "Kiss me. Please."

He couldn't erase the questions from her eyes, but he could kiss the lips she offered to his. He could give her, give them both, this moment. He could—and he would.

He bent his head and tasted heaven. "Johanna, my sweet Johanna, I think I've loved you forever. I've loved you and didn't even know you. I've been waiting for you. Only for you."

She looked up at him, shaken by the emotion in his voice, the pain she read in his face.

"Whatever happens, remember that I love you." He gripped her shoulders. "Promise."

She looked at his eyes, stricken now with fear rather than pain. "You're frightening me."

He released his grip and brushed his hands over her hair. "I'm sorry. That's the last thing I want to do."

"Tell me, Cade. Whatever it is, we'll face it together. There's nothing you can't say to me."

"I wish it were that simple."

A shiver raced down her spine. At the same time, the hair at the nape of her neck prickled. His fear was contagious.

Cade was the most deliberate man she'd ever met. Everything he did and said had a purpose. Why, then, was he having such difficulty talking to her?

Instinctively she knew it had something to do with her. But what? Her stomach pitched, and she placed a hand over it to calm the jittery feeling.

Cade drew her to him. "I love you. You have to believe me. No matter what happens." He took her face between his hands. "Will you do that for me?"

"Yes," she said softly, not understanding his urgency but frightened all the same.

"Promise," he ordered roughly. "You've got to promise."

Shocked by his intensity, she nodded. "I promise." She rubbed her cheek against his callused palm and relaxed when his grip on her gentled.

"I'm sorry. I didn't mean to hurt you." Tenderly, he stroked her jaw with his thumb.

"You didn't." She twisted in his arms so that his lips now rested on the curve of her shoulder.

"I don't deserve you."

"Don't say that. Don't ever say that." She held him tightly, as though she could ward off the demons chasing him. Whatever they were, she and Cade would fight them.

Together.

At last, he lifted his head. His eyes were bleak, but his lips had curved into the smile she was beginning to recognize. "You're a special woman, Johanna. But you know that already, don't you?"

She continued to hold him. Whatever was troubling him couldn't defeat them as long as they were together. She had to believe that.

"How'd I get so lucky?" Cade murmured.

"I'm the lucky one," she said, and knew it was true.

"Johanna Kellerman?"

A slightly stooped man with gray hair stood in her doorway. A banker type, she decided, panic coiling in her stomach. She didn't recognize him, but she'd kept her dealings to one man. There could be others at the bank that held the note on the ranch.

A dozen reasons for his presence flashed through her mind, each more awful than the next. Her note. He'd come to collect . . . ? Her mind rejected that. Her payments were current.

"Victor Wingate."

Carefully wiping her hands on her pants, she held out her hand. "Mr. Wingate. What can I do for you?"

"It's General Wingate. It's more like what I can do for you."

"I don't understand—" Her words died as he handed her a bank draft. She scanned it, her eyes widening at the amount. "Why?"

She hadn't believed in fairy tales for a long time, but a check like this might have her changing her mind. Even as she allowed herself a moment's fantasy of what she could do with the money, she was handing it back. "I don't know who you are, but no one gives away this kind of money for nothing. So I'm asking again. Why?"

A flicker of irritation ran across his face as he pushed a hand through his iron gray hair. A muscle twitched in his cheek, but it was his eyes upon which she focused. Gray like his hair, they were as cold as the wind that whipped down from the Colorado Rockies in mid-March.

"The money's to leave my sister alone."

"Your sister?" What did his sister have to do with her? Maybe the man was an escapee from an asylum. She took an instinctive step back.

A thin smile creased his lips. "Don't play the innocent with me, Miss Kellerman."

"I don't have time to play anything. So why don't you tell me why you're here?"

She resisted the urge to squirm under the scrutiny he subjected her to. Who was this man, and what did he want with her?

"You favor her," he said at last. "Around the eyes."

"Who?"

"You really don't know, do you?"

"Know what?" Impatience crept into her voice. She didn't like being questioned when she had no idea what the man was talking about.

On anyone else, the curl of his lips might have been a smile, but the twist of his mouth had her stepping back once more, seeking to widen the space between them.

"Trudy would have found you eventually," he said.

She had the impression he wasn't talking to her, but to himself, trying to accept something particularly unpalatable but inevitable all the same.

"Trudy?"

"Your mother. My sister."

"My mother died . . ." His words finally took on meaning. "My mother wants to see me?" Hope, anger, and fear fused together in an uneasy brew.

"She thinks she does. That's why I'm giving you this." He thrust the check back into her hands. "Stay away from her. She doesn't need the likes of you interfering in her life."

She took a minute to absorb his words. With a calm she was far from feeling, she tore the piece of paper into pieces. "Keep your money, Mr. Wingate. I don't need it. I don't want it."

He looked around, contempt in his gaze as he took in the shabby surroundings. "No?"

The faint sneer in his voice had her lifting her chin, but she held on to her temper. "No. If I decide I want to see my mother, no amount of money could keep me away." She asked the question uppermost on her mind. "How did you find me?"

"I wondered when you'd get around to asking that. It wasn't hard. All it took was money."

"You'd know all about that."

He nodded complacently. "I've known where you were for some time now. I've just been waiting for the right time."

"Right time for what?"

"The right time to make my offer. I heard you were thinking about expanding and thought you might need capital. The kind that doesn't need to be repaid."

"What makes you think I'd take your money?"

"You have a substantial bank note to pay back," he said, a distinct curl of mockery twisting the edges of his voice. "Your foreman is thinking of leaving to find a better-paying job. Your equipment is falling apart, your men understaffed."

How had he learned so much about her?

He must have seen the question in her eyes, for he smiled. "It pays to hire the best. I like to think I get what I pay for."

"The best?" The words had a small wisp of fear circling her heart.

"I believe you have a new man working for you?"

She nodded. Cade. The best thing to ever happen to her. Her breath jammed in her throat as his implication sank in. Wingate couldn't mean Cade. A heaviness in her chest told her to prepare for the worst.

"Larrabee always comes through."

Her nerve endings crackled while her mind ran through the implications of Wingate's words.

The sound of Cade's name on Wingate's tongue rolled ice through her gut. *Not Cade. It can't be Cade,* her heart screamed. *Please, don't let it be Cade.* She must have given voice to her prayers, for Wingate nodded.

Her throat tightened. She felt her hands growing clammy, fear gnawing at her gut.

She couldn't let Wingate see it. Instinctively, she knew he was the type of man to sense weakness and pounce on it. He needed to believe she was tough, in control, ready for whatever else he chose to throw her way.

"That's right. Cade Larrabee. He's worked for me for . . . oh, let's see, over ten years now. He served under me in the army."

He read the shock in her eyes. His lips lifted at the

corners in a travesty of a smile. "What's the matter? Did he fail to mention he worked for me? Don't feel bad. It must have slipped his mind."

At last she found her voice, and her faith. "I don't believe you." Her voice had risen sharply. She pressed her lips together, biting down on the lower one until she tasted blood. That steadied her, although her face heated, her throat shockingly raw.

Fear that he might be telling the truth tasted sour as vinegar in her mouth, but she forced the words through. "I don't believe you," she repeated, more calmly this time. She had only this man's word. Weighed against that was what she knew of Cade, his character.

He waved a careless hand in the air. "Of course you don't." His tone was gentle; his eyes were not. "Why don't we wait? I'm sure he'll be happy to tell you all about it."

She held on to her faith in Cade. Somehow Wingate had found out Cade was working for her and was now trying to implicate him. She didn't know this man standing before her, but she felt his coldness, saw the loathing in his eyes.

What she didn't understand was why.

She'd never met him before. Why did he hate her so? If his sister were her mother, that made them family. Why was he so anxious to keep them apart? She wasn't aware of asking the question aloud until she saw his hands clench around his cane. She took another step backward at the hatred that spilled from his eyes.

"Thanks to me, Trudy is a millionaire. Silver," he added. "Silver's king in Denver."

Understanding came slowly and with it, rage. "And you think I want part of it?"

The rasping sound coming from her throat startled her until she identified it as laughter, but the laughter had no mirth in it. It was as cold as the eyes of the man who stared at her with the same disdain he would regard a steaming pile of manure.

"Don't pull that virtuous act with me. Everyone wants more. Especially a little nobody like you who's out for everything she can get. You think I don't know how you got the Kellermans to leave you everything they had?"

For a moment she thought of the debts her father had left her. She didn't intend to share that with Wingate, though. She lifted her head proudly. "My parents gave me the most important thing of all. Love."

"Love?" He snapped his fingers. "That's all it's worth."

She saw him then for what he was: a pathetic excuse for a man who would never know the joy of loving and being loved. However much wealth he had accumulated, he was poor, would never be anything but poor in what mattered most. That gave her strength.

The idea that this man with his twisted views might be related to her filled her with revulsion. If his sister was anything like him . . . Johanna shook her head. He'd told her that Trudy was looking for her. Trudy couldn't be like her brother.

"My *parents*"—Johanna stressed the word—"gave me a home and love. That's all I ever wanted from them, all I ever expected."

His hoarse laugh disintegrated into a cough. A series of spasms shuddered through him.

Instinctively, she stepped forward to steady him, but he shrugged off her hand with a snarl.

She looked at him more carefully and noticed the telltale signs of age she'd missed before. The iron-gray hair showed traces of white; his shoulders were stooped. The hand gripping the silver cane quivered ever so slightly. But if his body showed signs of weakness, his eyes didn't. Cold and gray, they pierced through her, causing a shiver to skate down her spine.

Unconsciously, she straightened her shoulders. "We have nothing to say to each other. You can leave anytime."

He surveyed her with surprise, perhaps even admiration. "You've got a lot to say for yourself. I like that."

She doubted that. She doubted he liked anything or anyone who dared to defy him.

"I'll wait. I've got business with Cade."

The arrogance of the man was unbelievable. She was about to throw him out when the door opened.

"Johanna." Cade took in her ashen face and dropped the length of bridle he was holding. A premonition settled over him as he asked, "What happened?"

"I don't know. Maybe you can tell me." Her voice was even, her face expressionless.

He took a hard look at her. It had happened. Still, he hoped he was wrong. "I have to—"

For an instant, everything stopped, all movement, all sound, but for the pounding of her heart. It seemed unnaturally loud, and she wondered, wildly, if Cade and Wingate could hear its drumlike beat as well.

"What's the matter, Larrabee?" Wingate interrupted, stepping into view. "Haven't told her the truth yet?" He glanced from one to the other, clearly enjoying himself.

A tight knot coiled in her belly. At the same time, an icy sensation dribbled down her spine, causing her to shudder.

"Truth?" she repeated dully. She looked at the man who meant more to her than life itself. *Tell me he's lying,* she begged silently.

"Larrabee's one of my best men," the man who claimed to be her uncle told her, satisfaction evident in his smirk. "I sent him to find you, and find you he did."

Dread gripping her stomach, Johanna stared at Cade, willing him to deny it. Her eyes implored him to tell her it wasn't true, that it was all some horrible mistake.

He stretched out a hand to her before letting it drop. She watched as a kind of resignation filled his eyes. He had expected this moment to come, she realized in a flash of insight.

A taut silence hummed in the room, broken only by Johanna's choppy breathing. She felt as though a giant hand were squeezing her heart.

She didn't hurt yet, but she knew, somewhere deep where the truth would not be denied, that pain would come, and it would be arriving soon. She pictured a tornado, sweeping through the prairie, destroying everything in its wake.

Once, when she'd been ten years old, she'd witnessed a tornado, its destructive power ravaging everything in its path. She'd clung to her parents, feeling their helpless fury as they watched a lifetime of work shattered by nature's whim.

Afterward, they had picked themselves up and gone to work, rebuilding the ranch, stone by stone, railing by railing. Only now did she fully understand how they must have felt, to have their whole world wiped away in a fraction of a moment.

She stared at Cade, pinning him with her gaze. "You work for Wingate." It wasn't a question.

He didn't deny it. "I wanted to tell you."

There it was. The pain, slamming into her sooner than she'd expected, crueler than she'd imagined.

She felt her heart tighten as though a giant fist were gripping it, cutting off the air to her lungs. Bile rose in her throat. Her stomach churned, then clenched.

Her hands were clammy, her vision constricted, as though her mind were refusing to take in the details of her surroundings while it struggled with what she had just learned.

*Please,* she prayed silently, *don't let me humiliate myself by retching up the contents of my stomach.*

"You came here to spy on me, spouting a bunch of lies." Her voice faltered before she summoned the strength to continue. "Convinced me that you cared for me."

Cade lowered his eyes, and she knew she had found the truth.

"Is anything you told me true? The things you told me about serving in the war, your brother?"

"Everything was true. All of it. I never lied to you."

"You've done nothing but lie to me. How could I have been so stupid?"

"Johanna—"

"Were you lying last night, when you said that you loved me?" How she ever got the words out, she didn't know.

"No. I would never lie about something like that."

"But you would lie about everything else, is that it?" She scarcely recognized the venom-filled voice as her own.

"I should have told you sooner. I tried. Heaven only knows how hard I tried." He hung his head before raising it to meet her gaze once more. "I couldn't find the words."

Johanna sat with tense, aching muscles for long, agonizing moments. Misery clogged her throat, and she stared wordlessly at him. Her world spun, and she stumbled as she backed away from him.

Cade reached out to steady her, but she flinched at his touch. She thought she saw hurt in his eyes but decided she must have imagined it.

Breath whooshed into her lungs. A good sign, surely. It meant she was still alive despite the heartache that threatened to consume her.

"Johanna," he tried again. "It isn't how it seems. I know it looks bad, but—"

"Looks bad? Why would you say that, Cade? Just because you came here to spy on me. What were you supposed to do? Find out how desperate I was? What I would do to get my hands on my mother's money?" The words spilled from her mouth like dry, brittle leaves.

There was enough truth in her charges to cause his face to redden. "It wasn't like—"

"Dear heaven," she murmured. "You really thought that, didn't you?" She ended harshly, every breath coming in a ragged burst. All color drained from her face, and she feared she was going to pass out.

"Please, let me explain."

"Yes, Johanna. Let him explain," Wingate seconded. "Tell her how you were going to do it, Larrabee."

Contempt saturated the air.

"I can imagine," she said, dredging up a last bit of bravado from somewhere deep inside herself. "How would it go? Something like, 'Sorry, I just happen to have been sent here by your uncle to spy on you, maybe find enough dirt on you to keep you from looking for your mother'? When you couldn't find anything, your boss decides to offer money."

He flinched at her bitterness.

Wingate stepped forward. "She's a smart one, isn't she, Cade?" He favored her with an admiring look.

Johanna felt sick at his words. "Get out," she whispered hoarsely.

"You heard the lady," Cade told Wingate coldly. "Right now, I'd like nothing better than to throw you out. It's your choice. Make it while you still can."

Wingate stared at him. His breathing turned raspy and labored; a muscle twitched in his jaw. For a minute, she thought he was having a heart attack. Miraculously, his face cleared.

"I'll be back," he said. "When you've had a chance to think things over. Make no mistake about it. You're not getting Trudy's money."

She bit back a retort, knowing she would only play into his hands by allowing anger to overwhelm her. Instead, she turned her back on him.

With the slamming of the door, Cade spun her

around to face him. "You have to believe me. I never meant to hurt you."

"Believe you?" She looked incredulously at him. "I believed you once. I'll never make that mistake again." She folded her arms across her chest, tucking her hands under her arms to warm them, even though the temperature had spiked during the day.

Chilled by the lack of emotion in her voice, Cade hesitated. He couldn't leave her like this, no matter how much she wanted him out of her sight. She looked physically ill. Self-loathing overcame him as he realized he was the cause of it.

"Let me help you," he said and took her arm.

A wave of nausea lurched in her stomach. She grabbed for the back of the settee but couldn't make her hands work.

Cade caught her by the shoulders as lightheadedness overtook her.

"Don't touch me." She made a weak attempt to evade him but was too shocked, too weak, to shake away his hand, and she allowed him to help her to the settee. To her relief, he did not sit beside her but instead straddled the room's one chair, positioning it so that she faced him.

She tried to turn away, but his gaze impaled her own, forcing her to meet his eyes. "Say what you have to say. Then leave. Maybe you can catch up with your boss."

Cade winced. "Wingate was telling the truth, up to a point. He sent me to find you. I agreed."

"Why didn't he leave well enough alone? I wasn't looking for my . . . for the woman who bore me, then gave me away."

"Trudy wanted to see you. He wanted to make sure the two of you never found each other."

"Does he really believe I'd try to take her money?"

His silence was answer enough.

"As if I'd care. All I ever wanted was to know why she gave me away."

"I know that."

She crossed her arms over her chest, her eyes burning with tears she refused to shed. She wouldn't give him the satisfaction of witnessing that weakness. "Then why didn't you tell your boss that his sister's precious money was safe?"

His hands cupped her shoulders. "I tried. But Victor Wingate doesn't believe that someone might not be motivated by money."

"Like he is?"

Cade gave a short nod. "Like he is."

"That still doesn't tell me why my . . . mo—" —she stumbled over the word—"mother wants to see me after all these years."

"Trudy's not been well the last couple of years."

"She's not—"

He shook his head quickly. "She's not dying. But she has arthritis. I think she wants to have some time with you while she can still get around."

She was aware of gulping in air without releasing any, aware of her hands fisting so tightly that her nails dug into her palms. "So Wingate had you find me before Trudy could trace me?"

"Something like that. That was before . . ."

"Before what?"

"Before I fell in—"

Her snort of disbelief stopped him before he could complete the sentence. "I reported back to Wingate that I'd found you. He wanted me to find a way to . . ." He struggled to find the words that wouldn't destroy everything they'd shared.

"To get close to me. Right?"

His shoulders slumped as he realized there were no words. "Yeah. See what you were like. Before we told Trudy we'd found you."

"He never intended to tell his sister, did he?"

"No. I didn't know that when I started the job." Too late, he'd realized his mistake.

"The job. That's all I was to you, wasn't I? A job."

The bitterness in her voice was so sharp he imagined she could taste it.

"You know better than that."

"You were supposed to see what you could use to keep me away from my mother?" She spit out each word, like nails hammered into a coffin.

"It wasn't like that."

"No? What was it like? You didn't come here to find out what I was like? If I intended to go after my mother's money?"

She saw the truth in his eyes.

"That's how it started," he said in a low voice.

"And that's how it's ending. Tell me, Cade. What did you report back to your boss? Did you tell him that I spend my days working with horses and my nights trying to figure out how to meet payroll? Did you tell him that I get my hands dirty and that I like it? Did you—"

"Stop it."

The command took him by surprise as much as it did her. He held out a hand. "It wasn't like that. It was never like that."

"What was it like?"

"At first, it was only a job. And then—"

"Don't tell me. You fell in love with me." Scorn turned what should have been the most beautiful of words into something ugly.

The scorn in her voice stung but not as much as the pain he saw in her eyes. He deserved whatever she dished out. He waited.

"What? Don't you want to deny it?"

"I can't deny falling in love with you," he said in a low voice. "I wanted to tell you, but . . ." How could he explain being blackmailed without exposing his brother? "There's someone else involved, someone I owe more than I can ever repay."

The intensity in his voice halted whatever she'd been about to say. At the same time, his obvious emotion told her how much this other person meant to him. More than she ever would.

"I spun you that yarn about needing a job. I knew you needed a trainer."

At his words, she recoiled as though he had struck her. It had all been deliberate. He'd used her. And she'd let him. What a fool she'd been. After years of not letting anyone get close to her, she'd all but invited him into her life.

Something he'd said only now registered. "You knew that Bill Riedman had quit."

A flicker of emotion crossed his face.

Realization came, and with it, a fresh surge of anger. "You arranged it, didn't you? You managed to get Bill away from here and then showed up to take his place."

"It was the only way I knew to get close to you."

"You certainly knew how to work your way into my life." A tightness in her throat constricted her breathing as she remembered the day he'd appeared at the work site. At the time she'd thought it was too good to be true—a skilled trainer showing up just when she needed one. Now she knew she'd been right. It *had* been too good to be true. Just as Cade had been.

Nothing she'd believed about him was the truth. Nothing she'd believed about *them* was the truth.

"I wanted to tell you the truth. A hundred times, I wanted to, planned to. I even tried."

"Then why didn't you?" Despite her struggle to keep her voice steady, she heard the tremble in it. At the same moment, she felt every heartbeat in her chest. "You could have told me anytime."

"It wasn't my secret to share." At her silence, he asked, "What was I supposed to do?" The question held a bone-deep anguish, but she ignored it.

"Do you expect me to feel sorry for you?"

"No. I had just hoped for some understanding."

"It's not like me to fall in . . ." She swiped angrily at the tears that trickled down her cheeks.

"Love?"

" 'Love'? I hate you." Goosebumps raised on her arms as she realized what she'd said. "I've never said that before."

"Right now, I hate myself."

"At least we have something in common."

"I never meant to hurt you."

She hesitated. Maybe, just maybe, he meant what he'd said. Then she hardened her heart against any hint of softening. Even if he did show real remorse, that didn't change what she was feeling. She'd been lied to, used, and made to feel a fool.

How could she forgive that? How could she forgive him?

He pulled her to him, his hands clamping her arms to her sides. "You once said you trusted me, that you believed me when I said I loved you. Is this how you show it?"

She gave a mirthless laugh. Summoning all her strength, she pushed against him, but she was no match for him and he held her tight. "You'd do well not to use words like 'trust' or 'believe' with me. Coming from you, they don't carry much weight."

Her struggles grew more heated as she realized the danger of staying in his arms. She didn't fear he'd hurt her; no, the risk was far greater than that. The longer he held her, the more she remembered the tenderness of his touch, the sweetness of his kisses, the whispered words of love. She couldn't afford those memories.

Fear lent her strength, and she gave one last push. This time, she managed to free herself.

"Good-bye, Cade."

He reached for her, only to stop when she jerked back. "Johanna, if you'll give me a chance . . ."

He stepped back, taking a hard look at her lifted chin, the challenge that emanated from her eyes. He dropped his hand and found himself responding to her anger with a touch of his own. "You made me a promise once. Looks like you're no better at keeping your word than I am." With that, he stalked away.

He found refuge in the barn. His anger dissolved almost as quickly as it had erupted. She had every right to her anger. Unlike himself.

He watched the ranch house, saw the oil lamps extinguished. After waiting to make certain everyone was settled for the night, he started to work.

He'd made a promise to Johanna to finish framing the barn. It was the last thing he could do for her. Her pain had gutted him, shattering resolve and honor and every other quaility he'd once believed he had.

He worked steadily, finishing one wall, then another. When the framing was finished, he turned his attention to the existing barn. After shoring up sagging rafters, he then cleaned every stall with a ferocity born of guilt, as though every shovel of hay, every scoop of manure removed would somehow cleanse his soul.

It didn't work, of course. How could it? He'd betrayed Johanna in the worst way possible.

The horses remained quiet, accepting his presence with a calm that said they knew he was doing something for them. He spent an extra few moments with Sage. The aging mare gave a pleased whinny when he placed an extra helping of oats in her feed bag.

He kept at his self-imposed task until dawn worked its way between the rafters. He couldn't afford to linger. He looked about, a sense of accomplishment filling him even as he felt his heart splintering.

After stowing his few belongings in his saddlebags, he mounted his horse, and, with a final salute to the place that had become home in a way nothing else had since his ma had died, he rode away. He couldn't stop thinking of the pain reflected in Johanna's eyes, a pain he'd put there.

There was one thing he could do for Johanna and Trudy. Under the circumstances, it was the only thing he could do.

## *Chapter Eight*

As morning light forced its way into her room, Johanna felt as though her heart was shriveling in her chest. She swallowed back a sob. There'd be time enough for tears later. Right now, she had work to do. Her animals didn't care that her heart was crumbling to pieces.

She forced herself out of bed. A moan boiled up from her throat. At least she wasn't retching. She'd been a fool. She'd given her heart and her trust to a man who deserved neither.

She'd walked into it with her eyes open, ignoring George's misgivings about Cade and her own better judgment. She had no one to blame but herself. The knowledge didn't lessen her pain.

Never had she felt such pain, not even at the death of her parents, and a gnawing emptiness that she feared she might never be able to fill.

Except for her parents and George and Sarah, she'd

kept pretty much to herself, leaning on no one. It had taught her self-reliance at an early age.

In a few short weeks, she'd thrown all that away. What was worse, she'd tossed it away on a man who had lied to her, used her.

Too intent on helping her pa build up the ranch and then taking it over when he died, she'd had little time or interest for romantic involvements. Until Cade Larrabee had walked into her life.

A sponge bath and fresh clothes gave her enough energy to face the day.

"Hey, Johanna," George called from the porch of the house. "When did you finish framing the new barn?"

She looked at him blankly. "I didn't."

"Well, somebody sure did."

Sure he must be mistaken, she followed him into the barn to find the framing completed. The smell of fresh sawdust hung in the air, motes of dust catching the light filtered in through the high windows.

Fresh tears sprang to her eyes. Cade. He must have worked all through the night.

"It was Larrabee, wasn't it?" George asked.

Fortunately, he didn't appear to expect an answer. "He's one fine worker."

"I thought you didn't like Cade," she was surprised into saying.

"I said I didn't trust him. But that don't mean I don't 'preciate work like this. When did he find time to do it? He must have worked all night."

"He must have," she echoed.

"Where is he, anyway? I owe the man an apology.

Anyone who'd work all night to do this is all right by me."

She swallowed the wad of emotion in her throat. "He . . . uh . . . had to leave. A family emergency."

George looked puzzled. "I thought he didn't have any family."

"You thought wrong," she said shortly.

"Sure," he said, giving her a strange look.

"Sorry. I didn't mean to snap at you. I'm just tired." She managed a smile, hoping it didn't look as brittle as it felt. "I didn't sleep much last night."

"Maybe you ought to take a couple of hours off, get rested up. The boys and I can take care of things."

"No." Aware that she'd practically shouted the word, she lowered her voice. "I'll feel better once I get to work." The last thing she needed was time alone with her thoughts and regrets. She'd have a lifetime to spend doing just that.

"Whatever you say."

Aware of his scrutiny, she flushed.

He hesitated. "Johanna?"

"Yes?"

"Whatever's happened with you and Larrabee, I'm sorry. I know you cared for him."

She should have realized she couldn't fool George. Although she prided herself on being able to conceal her emotions, facing Cade's betrayal had punched holes in her defenses. "So am I."

Johanna threw herself into her work. Work had always provided a refuge for her in the past. Now, though, it proved as empty as her heart. Still, she kept at it.

Cade's work on the new barn had sparked a desire in

her and the others to spruce up the place. If she failed to find peace, at least she had the satisfaction of knowing the ranch had never looked better.

She went through the motions of working, her hands sure and competent. But her mind—and her heart—were with Cade.

Always Cade.

A week after Cade had left, Johanna was functioning. Just barely. Thoughts of Cade penetrated her nights as well as her waking hours, turning what sleep she managed to get into pain-filled dreams.

The solution was simple. She simply wouldn't think about him. Of course, ordering herself not to think about him resulted in her thinking of little else.

She thought of the weaving her mother had tried to teach her. She regretted now that she had never learned the skill, as she recalled the peace, the reassuring sense of continuity it gave her mother. *The patterns are the patterns of life,* her mother had said. *Cycles, repeating with the occasional variation, appear if you looked hard enough. You'll create your own pattern, different from mine, but no less important.* Her mother had been right. She had woven her own pattern.

Cade had taken the carefully woven fabric of her life, and with a few snips at the threads, had unraveled what she'd worked so hard to achieve. She had reached the point where she could admit that nothing would be the same for her. How could it be?

When her mother and then her father had died, she'd thought her life had come apart at the seams. Carefully, thread by thread, she'd rewoven it, forming another pattern, different but just as strong. Now she had to make yet another change, insert a different color into the complicated pattern she called life.

She'd fallen in love with him. What she did with that was up to her.

Tears spilled over and ran unheeded down her cheeks. For once, she allowed herself the luxury of crying. She cried for herself, for Cade, and for what might have been.

Wryly, she acknowledged that she had been—was—so in love with him that she could barely think straight. *When it happens to you, it'll hit hard,* her pa had told her. As usual, he had been right.

She tightened her belt another notch. She'd lost weight over the last week. Putting Cade out of her mind wasn't proving hard—it was proving impossible. But she wasn't a quitter. She'd find a way to live without him. After all, she'd spent the first twenty-seven years of her life without him.

She turned away from working with the horses, which normally brought her such joy. There was no joy left for her. She would leave the training to George and the others. Instead, she spent her time with the accounts. Perhaps as a punishment to herself?

Her musings were cut short as she saw George approach. The smile she forced faded abruptly at the scowl she saw on his face.

"You lose much more weight, you'll have to start wearing suspenders to hold your pants up." The innocent words scraped along her nerves.

She found a smile and pasted it on her lips. "I've lost a few pounds. It's nothing to fret about." The last came out sharper than she'd intended.

"It is to those who love you."

The quietly spoken words shamed her. George didn't deserve her short temper. He was a friend, the best she'd ever had.

"I'm sorry."

Awkwardly, he laid a hand on her shoulder. "It's all right."

She resisted the urge to squirm under his assessing look.

"It's him, isn't it?"

"I don't want to talk about him." It was anger she was feeling, she told herself, but she couldn't keep the pain from her voice.

"Maybe you need to."

"Since when have you started defending him? You never liked him. You said so."

"What I said is that I didn't trust him. He didn't look like a drifter. Turns out I was right."

"So?"

"So I saw the way he looked at you."

"What way?"

"The same way I look at Sarah, the way a man looks at the woman he loves."

Hope flickered within her, then died with disbelief.

"You're wrong," she said at last. "Cade doesn't love me. He may have cared about me a little, but love . . ." She shook her head.

"If he doesn't love you, honey, he put on a darn good show of it. A man doesn't look at a woman like that unless he's in love. I ought to know. I've felt that once in my life and look what happened." A smile broke through George's lined face.

She laughed, as she knew he'd intended.

"If we keep going like we are, we'll be out of the hole before the end of the year," he said.

She flashed him a grateful smile. George knew when to drop a painful subject. He'd said what he wanted to. Now he was giving her time to think about it.

"Yeah," she agreed. Unable to bear the inactivity of sitting at a desk, she stood and started to pace.

"You gonna be all right?"

*No,* she wanted to shout. *I'm not all right. I may never be all right again.* But she couldn't say that. Not even to George. "I'll be fine."

George gave her a look that said they both knew better.

So she summoned a smile, a pale imitation of the real thing, and feigned a yawn. "Guess I'm a little tired."

"I better get back to work," he said. "I got me some bridle mending to see to." George looked like he wanted to say more but took the hint and left.

Much as she tried to dismiss his words later that evening, she couldn't forget them. The notion that Cade loved her wouldn't vanish. Neither would the certainty that, despite everything, she loved him. How could she find the strength to stop feeling so much for him?

A deep loneliness swept over her. She swiped at a tear that fell down her cheek and closed her eyes to a grief she feared would remain with her for the rest of her life.

## *Chapter Nine*

When the letter came, she wasn't prepared.

Who was ever prepared for a letter from a stranger who claimed to be the woman who'd given her life twenty-seven years ago, and then had given her away?

Johanna stewed about it for hours before writing back, and hoped she hadn't made the biggest mistake of her life.

No, the biggest mistake had been giving Cade Larrabee a job. The flash of pain surprised her. Surely she should have started to heal by now, but the pain was there, as swift and sharp as ever. Maybe that was the way with love.

And with that admission, she knew the pain would forever be a part of her. She would learn to live with it, if for no other reason than that she had no choice.

With that acknowledgment, she focused her attention on her upcoming visit.

No law said she had to like the woman, Johanna reminded herself. She would meet with Trudy, and that would be the end of it. She'd remained detached; after all, Trudy had discarded her with no more thought than she'd have given to tossing out scraps for the hogs.

No, that wasn't fair, Johanna chastised herself. She didn't know why Trudy had given her up. She owed it to the woman to find out. What's more, she owed it to herself.

She told herself that she wanted only to meet the woman, but it was more than that. She longed for family. After the death of her parents, a hunger had grown inside her that never completely went away. It nagged at her in quiet moments and whispered to her during busy ones.

The hunger was a demanding, constant companion, and she knew the only way to appease it was to find answers to the questions that had plagued her for as long as she could remember.

The day she was to leave dawned gray and dreary, with a heaviness to the air that echoed the heaviness in her heart.

George volunteered to go with her, but she refused. "This is something I have to do on my own," she told him.

The stage trip to Denver wasn't nearly long enough. Not long enough to order her thoughts. Not long enough to school her emotions. Not nearly long enough to determine if she could do this.

An extra few coins and a smile for the stage driver convinced him to take her to the address Trudy had sent her.

"You gonna be all right, miss?" the driver asked.

Johanna settled her small hat more securely on her head. "I don't know."

The three-story brick house was set back from the

street, flanked by lush gardens replete with every flower imaginable. Everything about it hinted at wealth. She spared a moment to wish she had dressed in something other than a skirt, a shirtwaist, and a sadly out-of-fashion traveling jacket. Her sense of humor took over when she remembered she had nothing else.

After a moment's hesitation, Johanna rapped on the door. She had thought about this moment for most of her life. Now that it was here, she was afraid.

No, that wasn't right. She was terrified.

A capable-looking woman garbed in a black dress and white apron led her into a small parlor and then discreetly disappeared. Johanna took her time looking about the room, noting the delicate chairs, the fresh flowers, the softly faded rug. Late afternoon sunlight spilled through the upper balustrade.

Everything bespoke a quiet taste and elegance, much like the woman who sat on a plum-colored velvet settee. Trudy Wingate was small and delicately built. She was also crippled. Lines of pain were etched on her face, in her eyes.

Johanna watched as Trudy pushed herself up and moved unsteadily toward her, her hands gripping a gold-headed cane. Johanna longed to cross the room and save the older woman the trip that was obviously costing her, but she sensed it was important to Trudy that she make the journey on her own.

Johanna looked at the woman who'd given her life. Her resolve to remain detached vanished under the love—and hint of fear—she saw in Trudy Wingate's eyes.

The poignancy of the moment wasn't lost on her. One instant a woman has a baby and the next she gives up that same baby. Now that woman and her grown child meet for the first time.

"Johanna."

The voice cracked a trifle, and Johanna swallowed the sob that caught in her throat. Trudy placed a thin hand on her arm and gestured to the settee she had just vacated.

Slowly, they made their way, Johanna's arm wrapped protectively around Trudy's waist.

Once seated, Trudy leaned back and looked at her daughter. Tears filled her eyes. She dabbed at them with a lace-edged handkerchief. "I hope you'll excuse the tears of a foolish old woman. It's just that I've waited so long . . ."

Johanna felt tears spring to her eyes and blinked them back. "So have I."

"Then we have a beginning."

A beginning. Something to build on. She exhaled sharply.

"You too?" Trudy asked. At Johanna's blank look, she added, "Butterflies."

"A whole flock. Only they're storks."

Their mingled laughter forged a bond, and Johanna knew it was going to be all right.

A maid appeared, bearing a tray containing a china teapot, cups, and a plate of cookies.

Without thinking, Johanna served Trudy, then herself. She gave silent thanks to her other mother, the woman who had raised her, for teaching her how to properly serve tea even though such niceties were rarely practiced at the Double J.

"You're beautiful," Trudy said, sipping from a bone

china teacup. Steam from the hot tea wafted up behind her hand. "Even more beautiful than I imagined."

Johanna smoothed back her unruly curls and wrinkled her nose. "Pa . . . Henry Kellerman . . . used to say I was cute."

"Fathers always think their daughters are cute," Trudy said. "But now you're a beautiful young woman."

"I take after you." It was true, Johanna decided. Trudy's features were an older, faded version of her own.

Trudy touched her own hair, which was soft brown and streaked with gray. "Now you're being kind to an old woman."

Johanna shook her head. "You're not old."

Trudy placed a hand on her heart. "In here, I'm old. I've felt old ever since I gave you away."

Johanna heard the grief in Trudy's voice and longed to ease it. "You did what you thought was best."

"No. I did what my brother thought best. I wanted to keep you. You'll never know . . . I was young, barely sixteen, when I met your father. He was older, more experienced. He literally swept me off my feet. A few months later, I found myself with child and alone."

"He left you?"

"Without a backward glance."

The words were spoken without rancor, only a quiet acceptance.

"Our parents were already dead. Victor sent me away to an aunt who lived in Cheyenne. I stayed there until you were born." Trudy's eyes grew soft and dreamy. "You had a wisp of red-gold hair and the biggest eyes I'd ever seen. I fell in love with you as soon as I held you in my arms. I'll always regret that I let Victor convince me to give you up."

Her words eased a long-buried pain in Johanna's heart, and years of doubt and questions fell away. Emotion was thick inside her as she realized that Trudy had wanted her.

How many nights had she lain awake, wondering why her own mother had given her away? Now she knew. She couldn't find it in her to blame Trudy. She'd been frightened and faced with a decision no young girl should be forced to make.

"I'm not blaming Victor," Trudy said. "It was my responsibility. I never could stand up to him. He was always strong, forceful, even when he was a boy." She twisted her hands in her lap. "He told me the baby—you—would be better off with a mother and a father. I believed him." She raised her head to smile tremulously at Johanna. "You were happy, weren't you, with the Kellermans?"

Johanna looked at this woman who had loved unwisely. Another bond between them. Trudy had suffered. It was there in her eyes, pain-filled and pleading, in the hesitancy of her voice, in the trembling of her hands.

"Yes, I was happy. My folks—the Kellermans—were good to me. They loved me. And I loved them." She said the last with a trace of defiance. She wouldn't apologize for loving her adopted parents.

"I'm glad. I wondered. I'd lie in bed at night and think about you, praying you were happy."

"I was," Johanna said softly. She couldn't feel any bitterness toward Trudy. Once maybe, but no longer. "The past is over. We have a future in front of us."

"That's right. A future." Trudy's eyes glowed with the

radiance of happiness. "There's so much I want to tell you, to ask you." Tentatively, she reached for Johanna's hand. "If you'd like, maybe we can spend some time together before you have to return home."

"I'd like that," Johanna said, a catch in her voice. "I'd like that very much."

With a tensing of her shoulders, Trudy shifted positions.

Johanna winced inwardly at the suffering she read in Trudy's eyes. She manufactured a yawn. "If you don't mind, I'd like to lie down for a bit. The trip—"

"Of course. We can talk more at dinner." Trudy reached for her cane.

Before she could rise, Johanna was at her side, her hand gently cupping Trudy's elbow. She'd done it without stopping to think. Now she wondered if she'd rushed in where she wasn't welcome.

Trudy's grateful smile banished any doubts.

To her surprise, Johanna felt herself responding to the smile, not just with a smile of her own but with a warmth that suffused her entire body.

It was a step, a small one, but a step all the same to bridge the gulf of twenty-seven years.

A few moments later, she found herself shown to a beautifully appointed bedroom. A finely crocheted tester covered the four-poster bed. A polished mahogany bureau occupied an entire wall and held a silver brush, mirror, and comb. An adjoining water closet featured every luxury.

But none of the lavish surroundings mattered as Johanna hugged to her the knowledge that Trudy loved her, that she hadn't given her up willingly. With that understanding, years of self-doubt and unanswered questions vanished.

Johanna spent the next hour in her room, thinking about what she'd learned. She couldn't help comparing Trudy's home to the Double J. She wouldn't trade her home, with its humble furnishings, for any of the brocades and silks of Trudy's mansion. It seemed to have become the older woman's prison.

They spent a quiet evening talking, filling each other in on their lives. When the last of the dishes had been cleared away, Johanna felt Trudy's agitation. The time for hard talk had come. In a way she was relieved. Better to get it out of the way before it could cast a cloud over her visit.

Trudy led the way to her sitting room. When they'd made themselves comfortable and sipped at their tea, Trudy began. "I know what Victor did, what he tried to do. I don't know what to say, except that I'm more sorry than I can say. And so ashamed."

"You didn't do anything—"

"That's just it. I didn't do anything. I wanted to find you, so I turned to my big brother, just like I've done all my life. I let him take over, and because of that, I almost lost you again."

"It wasn't your fault," Johanna protested. "You didn't know."

"But I should have. When I first raised the question of trying to find you, I should have known Victor wouldn't go along with it. But I wanted to believe he'd changed. I wanted it so much that I let myself believe him when he said he'd help me find you."

"It's all right," Johanna said, pressing Trudy's hand.

"I've been a fool, but no more. You're here and I'm not letting you go."

Johanna shifted uncomfortably. "Trudy, I—"

"That didn't come out right," Trudy said quickly. "I sound like a silly old woman trying to hold on to the daughter she never had. I only meant, I want you to be a part of my life, to visit me whenever you can. If that's all right with you." The last was added in a wistful whisper.

"More than all right," Johanna whispered.

"Victor can't hurt us again. I think he knows that. Now that we have that out of the way, let's talk about you and Cade."

Johanna's breath caught in her throat. Would she ever be able to hear Cade's name without feeling a rush of grief? "What do you mean?"

"He came to see me a few days ago, told me what he'd done. He could have blamed Victor, but he didn't, said he accepted full responsibility for everything." Trudy paused as Johanna digested that. "It didn't take much to see that the man's in love with you." Trudy studied her daughter's face. "You're in love with him too, aren't you?"

The matter-of-fact way Trudy said the words convinced Johanna she'd be wasting her time denying them. "I was. Don't worry. It's over now."

"Is it?" Trudy gave her a shrewd look. "How does Cade feel about that?"

"I doubt he feels anything at all."

Trudy only smiled. "Except for being in love with you."

"I thought he was." Johanna winced at the flat words. "I was wrong."

"Were you?"

"Very wrong," she added in a low voice.

"I'm new at this mother business, but I've been around long enough to know that you don't stop loving someone just because he disappoints you."

Johanna recalled the pain she'd felt upon learning that Cade worked for Wingate. "He did more than disappoint me. He betrayed me. Betrayed you."

"I can see why you'd feel hurt, but betrayed?" Trudy shook her head. "If Cade made a mistake, it was one of judgment. He had a decision to make, and he did what he thought was right."

"Was it right to lie to me, to make me fall . . . to make me care for him?" Johanna flushed at the anger in her voice, but, to her surprise, Trudy didn't appear upset.

Her heart was proving stubbornly insistent in recalling every detail about Cade. The way his hair fell across his forehead when he threaded his fingers through it. The way a smile spread slowly over his lips before reaching his eyes.

"Did Cade tell you why he agreed to Victor's orders?" Trudy asked.

Johanna frowned as she tried to recall his words. "He said something about repaying an old debt."

Trudy nodded, as if she'd just confirmed something important. "That sounds like Cade." She looked thoughtful.

Johanna couldn't understand Trudy's defense of the man who had schemed to keep them apart. When she said as much, Trudy shook her head. "What did Cade say when you asked him why he stayed?"

"He said if he left, Wingate would only send someone else."

"He was right. My brother is nothing if not determined. He'd have sent another man, probably someone far more ruthless than Cade."

"Why didn't Cade tell me the truth when we started . . . when we found that we . . ."

"Cared for each other?"

A small nod was all Johanna was able to manage.

"Maybe he was afraid you'd send him away."

She thought about it. Trudy was right. She would have sent him away as soon as he'd told her the truth. And why shouldn't she? He'd used her, lied to her, and then had the gall to ask her to forgive him.

"Have you forgiven me for giving you up?" Trudy asked.

Johanna sensed Trudy didn't want an easy answer. "I don't know. I'm working on it."

"Have you wondered, then, why you're so certain you can't forgive Cade? My betrayal was far worse than his. I gave away my own child out of weakness. Whatever Cade did, he did for a far more noble motive. I'm certain of it. Can't you find it in your heart to forgive him?"

Forgive Cade? Trudy made it sound so easy.

Trudy laid a frail hand on Johanna's arm. "If you give him the benefit of the doubt, I think you'll see that he'd never willingly betray you. It was Victor's surprise arrival that complicated things. Otherwise, they might have turned out quite differently."

"Why couldn't he have just told me?"

"If Victor hadn't shown up when he did, I feel sure Cade would have told you in his own time."

"How can you be so sure?"

"He isn't an easy man, but he has his own code of honor."

Unwillingly, Johanna remembered Cade's promise that they'd finish framing the barn. He'd kept that, even though it meant working long hours every evening, hours she hadn't been able to pay him for.

After she'd ordered him out of her life, he'd stayed and worked through the night. Even George had been impressed by Cade's drive.

"You're too old for me to try to tell you what to do," Trudy said, a wry smile edging her lips. "But maybe you'll take some advice from a friend?" At Johanna's faint smile, she continued, "Pride makes a cold friend. So does loneliness." She paused. "I ought to know."

"Trudy . . ."

"Promise me you'll think about it?"

Johanna wanted to refuse, but the appeal in Trudy's eyes changed her mind. "I promise."

"Good." Trudy rose to her feet, accepting Johanna's quickly offered help.

"Tomorrow, maybe you'll indulge me in a dream I've had for a long time."

"If I can." She waited for the request, but Trudy only smiled.

"Tomorrow's soon enough."

The following day, Johanna found herself being fitted for a dress by a seamstress who came to Trudy's house. "I've never had a dress made just for me." She fingered the fine fabric. "It's beautiful. And much too dear." She had little experience with dresses, custom-made or not, but she recognized expensive material.

"You're beautiful," Trudy said, her voice husky. "It's perfect for you. Please, give me the pleasure of getting it for you."

Johanna wavered. Trudy's voice held such happiness, underscored by a hint of pleading, that she couldn't refuse. "Thank you. It's the most beautiful dress I've ever seen."

Trudy kissed her cheek. "No, thank *you.*" She reached to her neck, undid a string of pearls, and pressed them in Johanna's hands.

When Johanna started to protest this, Trudy turned a beseeching smile on her. "Please. Take them. For me."

"Do you always get your own way?" Johanna teased.

A faint shadow crossed Trudy's face. "Not always."

Instant regret filled Johanna at her thoughtless question, and she reached for Trudy's hand. "I'm sorry."

"Don't be. I have much to be grateful for. And having you here is the most wonderful gift in the world."

Johanna wondered what the future held for herself and Trudy. The only thing she knew for sure was that she very much wanted one.

*What about a future with Cade?* a small voice asked. Did she want one with him as well? She pushed the question to the back of her mind, to be dealt with at a later time.

Between Trudy and the seamstress, Johanna found herself agreeing to having three more dresses made.

Following the fitting, a maid served high tea. Reluctantly, Johanna declined seconds on the scones with clotted cream and jam.

Learning that Trudy had arranged a dinner with the son of a friend for the following evening had given Johanna more than one uneasy moment. The last thing she wanted was to have dinner with a strange man, no matter how attractive Trudy insisted he was. Her heart was still too bruised, her feelings too uncertain, to allow room for another man in her life. Seeing how important it was to Trudy, though, she'd given in.

Late the next afternoon, the seamstress paid another visit, this time with the first dress already completed.

"How did you finish it in so short a time?" Johanna asked.

The lady, no bigger than a sparrow, smiled. "Miss Wingate is a much-respected and very valued client." The seamstress helped Johanna slip into the dress, then fastened the row of tiny buttons. "It suits you," she said simply.

Johanna gazed at herself in the mirror. The amber silk flattered her coloring, bringing out the russet and gold in her hair.

Two hours later, Johanna descended the curving staircase, feeling slightly self-conscious in her new finery and her upswept hair, courtesy of Trudy's maid.

The look in Trudy's eyes erased any doubts about her appearance, however. "It will be a miracle if Betsy Bethune's son doesn't propose to you on the spot."

Johanna grimaced at the thought of the upcoming dinner. "I'd rather spend the evening with you."

"And forgo dinner with one of Denver's most eligible men?" Trudy's eyes glimmered with amusement and something more—a speculative look that had Johanna frowning.

"I'm not interested in men right now, eligible or not."

"Have you wondered why?"

Trudy didn't give her a chance to answer as she started discussing their plans for tomorrow.

"Are you sure you don't mind being alone tonight?" Johanna asked as they waited.

Trudy nodded emphatically. "I've been alone for most of my life. Besides, Betsy would never forgive me if you didn't go to dinner with her son." Trudy smiled mistily. "You look beautiful."

That night had set the pattern for the next week.

Despite Johanna's protests that she wanted to spend the time with Trudy, she had gone out nearly every evening, all at Trudy's insistence, each time with a different man. Trudy seemed to have an endless supply of friends with eligible sons or nephews, all of whom claimed to be eager to meet Johanna.

"My friends know the truth," Trudy had told Johanna. "They've known about you—my baby—for some time. Now I have the opportunity to show you off."

On her last night there, when she'd held firm to her desire to spend the evening with Trudy, Johanna touched the pearls at her neck. "Can I ask you something?" Without waiting for an answer, she plunged on. "I thought you wanted me to think about my feelings for Cade."

"I do."

The satisfied tone in Trudy's voice confirmed Johanna's suspicions. "All these men. You did it just so I'd compare them to Cade."

Trudy gave a mischievous smile. "What do you think?"

"That you're pretty sneaky."

"I've had a good teacher." The smile in Trudy's eyes dissolved at the reference to her brother.

Johanna bit her lip. The last thing she wanted to do was remind Trudy of Victor Wingate. Upon learning that Johanna was staying with his sister, Wingate had stormed into the house and demanded that Johanna leave. Trudy had stood up to him with a quiet dignity that filled Johanna with pride.

"No more," Trudy had said after the scene with her brother. "Victor's bullied me for the last time."

After that, there'd been no more contact from him.

"So, have any of these handsome young men stolen your heart?" Trudy asked, only a trace of sadness lingering in her eyes.

Her smile wry, Johanna pulled her lacy shawl around her shoulders. "I think you know the answer to that."

Trudy reached up to kiss her daughter's cheek. "I think you do too. Don't throw away a chance at love. It comes too rarely and, when it does, should be treated as a precious gift."

The following day, Johanna made the journey back to the Double J.

She was glad to be home. The ranch house looked small, the furniture threadbare, compared to Trudy's well-appointed house, but it was home. The sun had gone down, but dusk had brought no relief from the heat, though summer had slowly turned into autumn.

The days she'd spent with Trudy had been bittersweet, as she thought of the years they'd missed, the years they still had before them. She would always think of Jenny

Kellerman as her mother, but Trudy Wingate had given her life.

Already, she and Trudy had made plans to spend Thanksgiving together. They were working their way to becoming friends.

One thing was certain. She didn't intend to waste time with regrets. They had been given a second chance. Trudy had taught her something already: a chance at happiness was too precious to waste, too rare to toss away.

Like she'd done with Cade.

She pushed that thought to the back of her mind, not yet willing to examine what she felt for Cade.

While bailing hay with George the following day, a yawn escaped before she could clamp her hand over her mouth. She felt George's concerned gaze on her and summoned a smile.

"Still not sleeping well?" he asked.

"Well enough." Her answer dismissed the subject. Or it would have, she reflected, if George had let it drop.

"It's him."

She didn't bother denying it. Not to George, who was as close to a big brother as she'd ever have.

A night's sleep did little to banish her heartache. She had dragged herself from bed before dawn, pulled on clothes, and headed to the kitchen.

She'd hoped to make her escape before Sarah could corner her and force some food upon her.

"There you are." Sarah pointed to a plate of fried eggs, thick slabs of ham, and flaky biscuits. "Eat."

"I don't really feel like—"

Sarah laid a hand on the mound of her belly. "Do you want to upset a woman in my fragile condition?"

Johanna sighed and sat at the table. She couldn't fight Sarah. "You're a fraud."

With the ease of long friendship, Sarah took a seat as well. "You're right. Doc says I'm healthy as a horse." She patted her rounded middle. "Now eat and make one of us happy."

Johanna nodded and took a bite of egg. And another.

To her surprise, she discovered she was hungry, and finished every bite of food. She pressed a kiss to Sarah's cheek. "Thanks for caring."

Sarah shooed her off. "Get out there and boss my husband around while I tidy up in here."

Johanna headed to the barn.

"Hey, Boss. Great news. A new job." The grin on George's lips nearly split his face in half. "Chet Watson, you recall he bought the old Tyler place, stopped by. He has a stallion he wants trained." He grabbed her around the waist and swung her around. "We're on our way."

"That we are." She shook off her melancholia. She had a future to look to. If it didn't include Cade, well, she'd learn to live with that.

"Harvey Thompson said you're the best there is," Chet Watson said when she met with him the next day.

The job, training an inky-black stallion, was a dream come true. A pedigreed bloodline and a spirited nature promised to make it a pleasure to work with the eighteen-hand-high animal.

"Can you teach that black devil how to behave without breaking his spirit?" The affection in Watson's voice warmed her. He obviously loved the animal, however bad-natured he was. "He came with a mile-long name that I misremember most of the time. I call him Raven."

Johanna reached out to stroke the stallion's powerful neck. "He's a beauty. Don't worry. We know what we're doing," she added, unable to believe her good fortune. A job like this would add to the Double J's reputation, not to mention bolster her sagging bank account.

When she told the rest of the men about the job, they whooped with excitement. "This means a bonus for everyone," she said. She turned to George. "And a raise for you." She named an amount. "I know it isn't enough to keep you here forever, but maybe—"

"It's plenty." He tipped back his hat and swiped at his forehead with a sweat-stained kerchief. "You don't know how much I was hoping for something like this. Leaving you and the Double J was gonna be the hardest thing I ever had to do."

A little of the burden weighing on her heart eased.

The new job required every bit of skill and patience she possessed. She spent hours just talking with Raven, letting him grow accustomed to her voice, her presence. She hadn't forgotten the lessons she learned from Cade, and she fashioned a hood of soft fabric to slip over Raven's head.

Not until she was satisfied he would tolerate her touch did she attempt to put a bridle on him.

"Good boy," she said at the end of the fifth straight day of working with the animal. "Good boy."

She had so many dreams, so many hopes. With the

successes of the last few months, she dared believed she could make them happen. She only wished she had someone with whom she could share the joy of seeing her dreams come true.

Not for the first time, she thought of Cade and longed for him to be at her side. He'd appreciate the opportunity of working with Raven just as she did.

A yawning emptiness stretched before her. Alongside the emptiness was a terrible yearning, nearly crippling in its intensity.

It wasn't logical, that emptiness. They had known each other scarcely a month, but Cade had made himself a vital part of her life. That his absence should leave a gaping hole was understandable, but that the hole should be so large—and still spreading—was unfair.

She continued working with Raven until she could bear the sadness no longer. It hit her in waves, pulling at her until she felt as though she were drowning in it.

She handed the stallion over to George. He didn't ask for an explanation, and she didn't offer one.

## *Chapter Ten*

Cade slapped his hat against his thigh, sending out puffs of dust before rapping on the ornately carved door. He needed to know how Johanna was doing. To do that, he needed to talk with Trudy. He wasn't proud of himself, but it couldn't be helped.

When the maid ushered him into a small parlor, Trudy didn't look surprised to see him.

"You look like you've been trampled by a stampede," she said without preamble. The left corner of her mouth tilted upward, showing the slightest trace of a smile and erasing any sting the words might have inflicted.

He returned it with a wry one of his own. "You look wonderful." It was true, he reflected. Her eyes sparkled with life. The shadow of pain was still there, but it was now overshadowed by happiness.

"I feel wonderful," Trudy said. "And it's all because of you. You brought my daughter back to me." At the concern in his eyes, she gave a quick shake of her head. "Don't worry. I don't intend to play mother at this late date. It's enough that we've found each other, that someday we may be friends." She pressed his hand. "I owe you more than I can say." She expelled a breath that quavered in a way that warned him that there were tears behind it.

He shifted uncomfortably as the tears tracked down her cheeks. "I didn't do anything, Trudy. Johanna came to see you because she wanted to."

"You found her." Trudy's voice turned husky. "I'll never be able to thank you enough."

He was grateful when the arrival of the housemaid forestalled any further expressions of gratitude. He sipped tea, picked at sandwiches no bigger than the palm of his hand, and talked of other things.

Cade made a pretense of eating until the question uppermost in his mind would no longer be denied. "How is she?"

The smile that parted Trudy's lips wasn't what he expected, but nothing that had happened since he'd accepted the job to find Johanna had been what he'd expected.

Her eyebrows winged up. "Why don't you ask her yourself?"

"You know why," he said in a low voice. "She hates me." The sourness in his gut had turned to an ache.

Trudy's smile widened. "I've always thought you were an intelligent man. Don't disappoint me now."

"Maybe she doesn't hate me. But I sure don't head her list of favorite people."

"How do you know?" Trudy asked reasonably. "Have you asked her?"

Hope flared in his chest, only to die again as he remembered the bitterness in Johanna's voice when she'd ordered him out of her life. "What're you saying?"

"Hurt sometimes makes us say things we don't mean. Even to the person we love the most."

Love.

At one time he'd believed it had no place in his life. Then he'd met Johanna. Her love had reached out to wrap itself around him, and he'd allowed himself to hope.

He wanted to rail at Trudy for causing that hope to spring to life again when he knew it had no chance of fulfillment, but the genuine caring he saw in her eyes wouldn't allow him to vent his anger.

"You do love her, don't you?" she asked.

Why pretend? "This is a first for me. And the last." He reached for Trudy's hand and pressed it between his own. "I'm glad you're happy," he said, meaning it. "You deserve it."

"So do you. I told Johanna something, but I don't think she heard me. She was hurting. Reach out and embrace life with both hands. If you don't . . ." Her shrug was eloquent.

She didn't finish. She didn't need to.

By mutual consent, they turned the conversation to other topics. Though he longed to hear more about Johanna, he wasn't sorry to drop the subject of his feelings for her. Trudy saw far too much, and right now his defenses were in tatters.

He was still mulling over what Trudy had told him when her voice interrupted his thoughts.

"I've watched you for a long time, Cade. You don't

give of yourself easily. You remind me of a wolf, always watching out for his pack, but never really part of it."

He nodded shortly.

Working things out on his own was so ingrained that he'd rarely questioned the practice. He'd always figured it was the right thing to do. Now he wasn't so sure.

"You're accustomed to going your own way, explaining to no one, even when it would clear things up between you and the woman you love."

"I don't—"

The look she gave him put a halt to the rest of the lie.

"Johanna needs you. What's more, she loves you. Don't you think it's time you told her the truth? Like how my brother forced you to spy on her."

"You know about that?"

"I know you'd never agree to something like that unless he had a powerful hold on you. Probably something to do with protecting someone you love."

He looked at her with new respect. There was more to Trudy Wingate than he'd reckoned.

"Tell me," she ordered softly.

Strangely, he found himself doing just that.

Trudy listened, nodding occasionally while he recounted the story. "So he threatened to tell the authorities about your brother. How long are you going to keep paying for a mistake a green boy made more than a dozen years ago?"

It was the same question he'd asked himself over and over during the last few weeks.

"Victor is my big brother, but I'm not blind to his faults. I allowed him to talk me into giving away my child, and I've regretted it every day of my life. Don't make the same mistake." She waved her hands impatiently at his protest. "You know what I mean. If you love Johanna, tell her."

"Don't you think I tried?"

The words were wrenched from him, and only then did he realize he'd shouted them.

Trudy didn't appear offended by his lapse in manners. He could have sworn he saw a hint of a smile chase across her lips before she said, "Then it's up to you to make her believe you." She paused for a moment and eyed him shrewdly. "Or won't your pride let you?"

He winced at the truth in the rebuke. The lady didn't spare her words—or his feelings. Apparently, she had some of the general in her after all.

When Johanna had refused to listen to him, he'd let her get away with it, disappearing from her life like a whipped dog with his tail between his legs.

"The truth hurts, doesn't it?" Trudy asked gently.

"Yeah." He managed a smile. "Yeah, it does."

"I'm sorry. Hurting you is the last thing I wanted to do, especially when you . . ." She dabbed at her eyes with a lace-trimmed handkerchief.

"Trudy, you don't have to—"

"Please, let me finish. You've given me back my life." She leaned across the table to brush a kiss against his jaw. "Whatever happens between you and Johanna, I hope you will remember that I'll always be grateful for what you did."

After taking his leave, Cade replayed his conversation

with her. What if she were right about Johanna's feelings for him?

He owed it to her—and to himself—to find out.

The husband and wife Cade had arranged to care for Noah were compassionate and saw to his every need. For that, Cade was grateful. It shamed him, though, that he had to force himself to visit his own brother.

The visit wasn't something he'd planned, but after talking with Trudy, he knew he needed to find a way to set to rest the ghosts of the past.

He found Noah in the front room of the ranch house, gazing out the window into the distance.

When he saw Cade, he smiled. The smile died when Cade failed to return it. "What's wrong?"

"Anything wrong with wanting to see my big brother?"

"No. If that's all it is."

Cade backed away from the reason for his visit and talked about other things, all the while sensing Noah's impatience, until his brother held up a hand.

"You've talked, I've talked, so why don't you tell me why you're really here?"

Cade looked at the brother he'd idolized, then pitied, and finally accepted as simply a man with human frailties, and that's when the realization hit him. Noah didn't need his protection any longer.

Lines of pain grooved his face. With the pain, though, came strength. It was that to which Cade had been blind. Perhaps he'd needed to be needed. Whatever his reasons, it was plain Noah didn't need, or want, someone to shield him from life.

Noah uttered something crude after Cade told him of

Wingate's blackmail, even though the story he told wasn't the full one. "You see these?" He pulled back the blanket covering his lap and pointed to the stumps of his legs.

For his brother's sake, Cade had learned not to flinch at the sight.

"I lost them because I was running away. Not because of some act of bravery, like the medal says. And it's time I started owning up to it.

"Little brother, you need someone to give you a swift kick in the rear. I'd do it, but I haven't got the equipment." Noah laughed, a rich, full sound that had Cade joining in. "You've got a blind spot about me." He spaced the words out. "I ran in the face of enemy fire. It wasn't anyone else's fault. It was mine. Only mine."

Cade balled a fist into his open palm. "You lost your legs, almost lost your life. You didn't deserve what Wingate could do to you."

"Who else should pay for my cowardice? It happened. And I'm not so bad off." Noah slapped the arm of the wood and cane wheelchair Cade had purchased for him. "Now let's talk about what you are guilty of."

Wary, Cade raised his head.

"It's been more than twelve years and you still treat me like the invalid you think I am."

Cade wanted to deny it but recognized the truth in the charge. "What do you want me to do?"

"Stop." The vehemence in Noah's voice shook Cade. More mildly, Noah added, "I appreciate all you've done for me, but it's time I started standing on my own two legs." He glanced down. "Figuratively, of course."

The dry note in his voice drew a reluctant laugh from

Cade. Cade clapped his brother on the back. "Someone from the War Department is probably going to be paying you a visit."

"I know. In a way, it'll be a relief. I've carried around a load of guilt for more than a dozen years.

"Now that we've straightened me out, let's talk about you." Noah subjected Cade to an intense scrutiny, a slow smile spreading across his face. "You met someone special."

Noah's blunt statement startled Cade into asking, "How do you know?" He'd meant to ease into revealing that he'd met the woman he intended to marry. Instead, Noah had already figured it out.

His brother snorted in exasperation. "I can't walk. That doesn't mean I'm blind. It's right there on your face."

Noah's legs might be gone, but everything else was working just fine.

"What's she like?" Noah asked.

"She's beautiful, smart, stubborn—"

"Do you love her?"

"Yes."

"Does she love you?"

That one was tougher to answer. "She did. I'm not so sure anymore."

"You made a mess of things," Noah guessed.

Cade gave a rueful nod. "Yeah."

"Want to talk about it?"

He found himself wanting to do just that. The story came out in bits and pieces. He didn't spare himself in the telling.

A tuck furrowed itself between Noah's brows. "You

agreed to spy on the woman and ended up falling in love with her?"

"Yeah."

"And now she despises you."

"I don't know. I thought she did. I'm hoping I was wrong."

"Go to her, convince her she's the only woman for you, and beg her to forgive you." Noah slapped his brother's arm. "Now get out of here so I can get back to work. You've got a lady to see."

"Do you want me—"

The look in Noah's eyes was enough to stop Cade's offer of help. "Whatever happens, I can deal with it."

After giving his brother a friendly shoulder bump, Cade turned to go.

"Hey, Cade?" Noah called.

"Yeah?"

"When you square things with your lady, don't forget to invite me to the wedding."

It wasn't that she'd buried herself in work; it was that work buried her. A horse had torn its leg on barbed wire. A cow had developed mastitis. Each took time. Each took energy. She was grateful she had both to give; even more so, she was grateful these problems forced her mind away from others.

She pushed her way through the day by sheer force of will, and if she gave in to the heartache that was never far away, no one knew. By the end of the day, she could swear she heard her feet weeping. Nineteen hours without a break.

The success on the ranch she'd longed for was close

enough that she imagined she could reach out and grab it. What had seemed so important months, even weeks ago, though, had faded in significance compared to what she had lost.

Cade. And a chance at a lifetime with him.

He had filled the empty places in her life, places she hadn't even known existed, until he'd shown her. A soft warmth stole over her as she remembered the gentleness of his kisses.

She was feeling stronger, Johanna reflected. She rarely thought of Cade anymore. Her lips quirked in a derisive smile. No more than twenty or thirty times an hour, at any rate.

The pain had mercifully blunted to a dull ache. She no longer feared it would rip her apart. Of course she had moments of missing him, but they were getting fewer. Definitely fewer.

Yes, she congratulated herself, she was handling it well. Another week, two at the most, she'd hardly spare a thought for him. And she tried to the awful hollowing pain that had dogged her these weeks without him.

The expectation shouldn't have left her feeling so unhappy. Her work with Raven was a joy. She should have been celebrating.

But some days, like today, when the sun blossomed through the clouds with fierce determination, when the air was heavy with the scent of freshly turned earth, when the birds sang so sweetly, it was difficult to forget Cade. He had come into her life just as the weather had hinted of the approaching fall. And he had left when the season was ripening to its fullness.

If she felt tears prick her eyes occasionally, well, it

was the hay. She certainly didn't need to apologize for that. Funny, she'd never been bothered by hay before, but there was a first time for everything.

A first time for falling in love.

She squashed the thought as soon as it formed, but she was too late. Memories of Cade assailed her. She let them have their way. Maybe if she unleashed them, they'd lose their power over her—and maybe the moon really was made of green cheese.

The memories tumbled together, one on top of the other. The two of them working a frisky colt together. Sharing a sandwich. Sneaking away to spend a few moments together. She examined each mind-picture with painful thoroughness.

Why couldn't she let them go?

*I love the man.*

*Admit it.* That done, she decided she felt better. Now if only she could convince her heart to let him go, but it was proving more stubborn than she anticipated. It clung to the fantasy she'd conjured up of her and Cade making a family together.

The sweetness she wanted to feel was tainted by barbed edges, as sharp as the wire that fenced off the land. Foolishly, she'd believed that love was unblemished. She knew different now.

Her memory stirred, and image upon image appeared. The gentleness of his hands when they framed her face. The strength of his arms when he held her. The warmth of his lips pressed against her own.

Impatient with her musings, she closed her eyes, willing the memories away. It didn't matter when it had happened. Or how.

Or why.

Life had played a cruel trick on her by allowing her to fall in love with the right man who believed he was all wrong for her.

If only . . .

She shook her head. "If-onlies" were futile; more than that, they were dangerous. They encouraged you to think about the might-have-beens. Her breath caught in a tiny sob. Might-have-beens had no place in her life.

Perseverance, hard work, and sheer will had gotten her this far when all the odds had been against her.

Her pa wouldn't have much sympathy for her head-in-the-sand attitude, she thought. He believed in meeting life head on. "Troubles grow smaller when met with one's eyes open," he was fond of saying.

The truth was, she was miserable. It had been the longest week Johanna could remember living through. If you could call this living.

Her parents had raised her to believe in herself, in her abilities. The independence they had instilled in her had served her well. Until now.

She functioned automatically, going to work, to bed, and back to work again.

All the joy had vanished from her world and, for the first time in her life, she dreaded getting up and facing each new day. Not even her overwhelming grief after losing her parents equaled the heartache she was experiencing now.

The way she had succumbed to Cade's last kiss was a constant rebuke to her. Even knowing he had betrayed her, she still wanted him, still loved him.

Images of him flickered through her mind. His patience during the long vigil over Sage. The sense of humor that surfaced at odd moments. She feared she would always judge other men by him, and she was very much afraid that none would measure up.

She needed Cade. She needed him to love her as she loved him. She needed his arms around her, his lips upon hers, his strong presence.

Unbidden, tears flooded her throat. Ruthlessly, she swallowed them.

She hated tears. Tears never helped. Tears never changed the world. Tears certainly hadn't brought back her parents.

And tears wouldn't bring back Cade.

## *Chapter Eleven*

"Johanna, your mind's a thousand miles away," George said when she handed him the wrong length of board for the third time in a row.

In between training Raven and keeping up with other chores, she and George had been working feverishly to finish the barn. Cade had given her a good start. It was up to her to complete it.

"Why don't you take off early?" George suggested. "We're pretty much done here. I can finish up whatever's left."

She lifted her gaze. The perfect autumn day beckoned to her. "Thanks."

He seemed about to say something, but only squeezed her shoulder. Grateful for his understanding, she gave him a quick smile and headed out to the grove of aspen bordering the property.

The sun's warmth lulled her into settling back against a tree. Her legs stretched out in front of her, she folded her arms behind her head. A soft breeze tickled her cheek. She'd rest here for a moment only, just long enough to gain the energy to go back to work.

She knew George was worried about her. It wasn't like her to take off early, even with his encouragement, but then nothing she did or felt lately was normal. Her lack of energy today was only one instance of many. She wanted to blame it on the heat, but she knew better.

Cade.

It had been almost a month since she'd ordered him from her life. The thought caused a strangled sob to catch in her throat. She wondered, not for the first time, if she'd judged Cade too harshly. Maybe she should have given him a chance to explain. It was too late now. Even if she wanted to find him, she had no idea where to start.

It was time to get on with life, she chastised herself. Cade was gone. The sooner she dealt with that, the better off she'd be.

As she sat, she heard a shrill cry from high above. She looked up to see a hawk circling. She watched as another hawk joined the first, the great birds' wings fan in perfect symmetry, catching the air currents, then riding them higher and higher. Their high-pitched caws pierced the air.

Hawks mated for life, she remembered her pa telling her. She closed her eyes and wished for her heart's desire.

Impatient with the melancholia that overtook her at odd times during the day, she wiped her hands on her trousers. What she needed was to get back to work. There were fences to check before cold weather set in, bales of hay to stack, stock to feed.

A movement in the woods caught her attention. She stopped, staring as a familiar figure took shape.

For a moment, she thought she was imagining it. Cade was there. Standing in the grove of trees flanking the house, his hair glinting in the sunlight, he was more handsome than ever.

Sights and sounds imprinted themselves on her mind, informing her that this was a momentous slice of time. As though she would need any such reminder. The wind in the trees. The distant cry of the pair of hawks, wheeling and turning through the Colorado sky.

A confusing tangle of emotions swirled inside her. Abruptly, it vanished, and everything became clear.

Who was she trying to deceive with all her talk about being over Cade? She wanted him, loved him, as much as she ever had. Seeing him now, she knew she always would.

Maybe it was time she started listening with her heart, she thought, remembering Trudy's words.

She felt her smile bloom from the inside out. She started walking, slowly at first. Her pulse quickened as her pace picked up. Then she was running. His arms opened. She didn't stop, didn't question, didn't think.

And then she was there. In his arms. His lips on hers. She knew it didn't matter how he'd come into her life. Or why. All that mattered was that he was there, that they loved each other.

Love didn't question; love accepted. And that was what she intended to do.

How long they stayed there, locked together, she didn't know. Didn't care. Minutes, hours—they were all the same.

"Cade—"

"Johanna—"

Her knees threatened to buckle, her heart started to flutter, and she knew she was blushing. She looked at him with sudden shyness. "You first."

"No, you."

"I'm sorry." As soon as she said the words, she felt a weight lifting from her heart. "I should have trusted you."

"I'm the one who's sorry."

She silenced his apology with a quick kiss. "It doesn't matter anymore. You're here."

"For as long as you'll have me."

"How long is forever?"

In answer, he gathered her into his arms again, kissing her with such intensity that she wondered how she'd ever doubted his love.

"You're sure?" he asked when he released her only enough that he could see her face.

"More sure than anything I've ever been in my life." She heard the whoosh of relief as he let out a breath. "How about you? Are you sure you want to get hooked up with a woman who wears manure instead of lemon verbena?"

He make a production of sniffing behind her ear. "I always liked the smell of manure."

"I wear men's clothing seven days a week. When I'm working, I forget what time it is, sometimes what day it is." She knew she was babbling, but she couldn't seem to stop herself. "I—"

"Talk too much." He kissed her again, a brush of lips that had her wanting more. "It's time I told you about Wingate."

"You don't have to." A man like Cade, who wore honor as easily as he did buckskins, would never agree to do what he'd done unless he'd had a compelling reason.

"I owe you an explanation."

"You don't owe me anything."

He cradled her chin in the curve of his thumb and forefinger. "I want to. I have to."

She recognized the thread of determination running through his voice. She didn't want to hear about the hold Wingate had over Cade. That was the past. But she sensed no amount of talking would convince him otherwise.

"It has to do with your brother, doesn't it?"

He released her chin, rubbed a hand over his jaw. "Victor Wingate was my commanding officer in the war. When he was transferred west, so was I."

"What you told me about being a soldier—"

"Was the truth."

"And after?"

"I continued working for Wingate after I resigned my commission. I did special jobs for him."

"Special jobs?" Was that what she had been?

He shook his head, apparently reading her mind. "You were never a special job. Not in that way. Not from the first time I saw you. But you were special."

"I don't understand."

"You were different, right from the start. When I first saw you, I knew this was going to be different. I tried to tell myself nothing had changed. That you were an assignment and nothing more.

"But something I never expected happened."

"What?"

"I fell in love with you. I wanted to walk away from the job. From the old man. From everything. But I couldn't leave."

She waited.

"I told you about Noah."

His brother.

"All the time we were growing up, he was my hero. He could do no wrong, at least not in my eyes. He was the one who held us together after our ma died. When he volunteered, I begged to go with him. He told me I was too young and left me with an aunt. He went ahead because he believed in what he was doing.

"Despite all the misery he witnessed, he didn't let it get him down. Not at first anyway." The pain that filled his eyes had her reaching for him. "When he came home without his legs, I tried to make everything right. But it didn't work.

"Noah started taking laudanum, got so where he couldn't get through the night without it. It got worse until I refused to let him take it. He hated me for it. For a long time, he refused to even see me."

She waited, knowing there was more to come.

"The last few years, things have been better. Noah seemed happier, more at peace with himself. I thought that things were finally coming together for him."

Seeing what it was costing Cade, she laid a hand on his arm. "You don't have to tell me any more."

He squeezed her hand and smiled faintly. "When Wingate told me what he wanted, I refused. Something about it didn't feel right. That's when he pulled out a letter. It was from the War Department. He must have been saving it for years, something to use when I didn't toe the line. I don't know how he got hold of it."

She was scarcely aware of holding her breath. Cade seemed to have slipped into the past, his eyes distant and unfocused.

"It said Noah was a coward. That he lost his legs when he was running from enemy fire, in the same skirmish that earned him the medal for bravery.

"At first, I couldn't believe it. I told Wingate it was nothing but a pack of lies and what he could do with it."

"Maybe you were right and it wasn't true."

"He pulled out a bunch more papers, backing up what the letter said."

"Why didn't the man who wrote the letter do anything about it?"

"He died before he ever had a chance to take it any higher. I kept telling myself that Noah couldn't have lied all these years about what happened."

"I wish you'd have told me. We could've worked it out together." She'd thought she'd known what it was to long to spare someone you deeply loved from pain, to want to ease a burden from his shoulders. Now she understood that she didn't know the depth of that need.

Just as she would have given anything to spare Cade the anguish of his choice, he had tried to spare Noah.

Sometimes it couldn't be done, not just because it was impossible, but because that experience was a part of who that person had become. Would she have wanted Cade to be any different?

No.

"So do I," he said with a heartfelt sigh. "A thousand

times, I wanted to. I've never been blackmailed before. Once you're in, you feel like you can't dig yourself out. I kept trying and only dug myself in deeper."

Her hand found his. "It's over. What happens now? With Noah."

"I went to see him, told him what Wingate was threatening."

"What did he say?"

"That it was time to tell the truth. He said he always knew it would come out sometime. He sounded almost relieved. Like it was something he'd wanted to do for a long time."

Wingate had played upon Cade's loyalty to his brother. She had known his loyalty ran deep, especially to the brother he loved more than his own life.

She swiped at her eyes with a balled-up fist, but the tears came anyway. She cried. For Noah. For Cade. For herself. "It wasn't your fault," she said at last, "what happened to Noah."

"I've finally figured that out." He touched her wet cheeks, brushing them dry with his thumbs.

"You told me once to let go of the past," she said softly. "It's your turn now. It's time to let go."

He brought her hand to his lips. "You're right. Maybe now I can. I went through life doing my job but never really caring for anyone, except Noah, since I got discharged. I thought all that had died a long time ago—at least for me." The warmth in his eyes sent waves of longing through her. "Until I met you."

"What will you do now?"

"I've put away most of my salary over the last ten years." His lips quirked into a tight smile. "Not much to spend it on except a small spread I bought for Noah. I was thinking of maybe going into business."

"What kind of business? Maybe I could help."

"Maybe you could. What I'd really like to do is to put it into a ranch." He cocked his head to one side. "Do you have any ideas?"

His face was serious, but she saw a smile lurking at the edges his mouth.

Her lips curved into a matching one. "I just might have one or two."

"Good."

"I've been thinking about taking on a partner." She drew her brows together, pretending to consider the matter. "Of course, it'd have to be the right partner. Someone who knows his way around horses. Someone who can see a job through from start to finish."

"Did you have anyone in particular in mind?"

"Someone very particular."

"Anyone I know?"

Her eyes shone. "You. And me. Together."

"You mean it?"

"More than I've ever meant anything in my life." Overwhelmed by the joy flowing through her, she started to cry.

"Hey, none of that," he chided and caught a tear on the pad of his thumb. His hand closed around hers. "Partners."

"Partners," she agreed through her tears.

"A partnership should be sealed."

A tiny frown stitched grooves at the corners of her mouth. "You mean a contract—"

"I mean this." The kiss was everything she'd dreamed

about during the long weeks they'd been apart, and she felt wrapped in a warm cocoon of happiness.

He wouldn't be an easy man, she thought. Never easy. His pride and honor demanded too much of him for that. But he would love her with passion and energy and would expect the same from her.

"This is a lifetime deal," he warned her. "Permanent and binding."

Everything within her became hushed with joy at the love she saw in his eyes. "You drive a hard bargain," she whispered. Her throat ached, straining to hold her trembling heart.

"I'm not bargaining," he said, his strong voice sounding suddenly vulnerable. "I'm begging. Spend the rest of your life with me, and I promise to love you as you've never been loved before."

It was no hardship at all to agree.

## *Epilogue*

Cade had spent the last month in the nation's capital. He'd stood by Noah during the painful hearings, and, later, cried with him.

The trip home, first by train, then by stage, was a healing time for both of them. They talked as they hadn't in years. For the first time in too long, Cade really listened to his brother.

To his shame, he realized he'd shied away from spending time with Noah. The anguish of looking at his brother, at what he'd lost, had been too much.

No longer.

"I've made peace with this," Noah said, gesturing to the blanket covering the stumps of what had been his legs. "Don't you think it's time you did too?"

Tears stung Cade's eyes. He groped for Noah's hand. Something passed between them. A new understanding. A respect based on honesty. A deepened bond that had waned over the last years.

When they reached the small ranch outside of Denver, Cade wanted to stay on for a few weeks.

Noah refused. "You have a lady who misses you." When Cade had hesitated, Noah punched his shoulder. "Go. I have everything I need. I think I'll be sleeping a whole lot better."

Cade had hugged his brother and knew they'd both come a long way. After making sure Noah was settled in, Cade made the trip to the Double J with a heart lighter than it had felt in years.

He found Johanna and George working in the corral with another inky-black stallion. Horse and woman made a beautiful sight. He took in every detail, the glisten of sweat upon the animal's flanks, the determination in the jut of Johanna's chin.

The stallion had met his match in her.

"You've a feisty way with you, but underneath I know you're a sweetheart," she said. "Now, show me what you learned."

As though to disprove her words, the stallion gave a sharp whinny and reared up on his hind legs. After giving a chastising slap to his neck, she put him through his paces, then patted him approvingly. He nuzzled her neck.

When she saw Cade, she turned the reins over to George and ran to him, wrapping her arms around him.

His entire being was centered on this one moment, this one woman. He cupped her face and kissed her. When he lifted his head, he saw tears in her eyes. "Are you crying?"

She swiped at the tears that trailed down her cheeks. "Only because I'm happy."

After long minutes, they broke apart.

"Tell me," she said.

Cade's expression sobered. "Noah made a full confession. The War Department stripped him of the medal and issued a dishonorable discharge, but they won't be pressing charges."

"That must have been hard." She reached for his hands. "On both of you. I'm glad it's over."

"Me too."

"All you have to do now is bring Noah here to live with us."

"You'd do that? Have him live with us?" He'd hardly dared dream of that, of bringing Noah to live with them.

"He's your brother. Of course I want him here. Trudy's promised to come for Thanksgiving. I'm hoping she'll stay through Christmas, maybe even longer. We'll make it a real family time."

He kissed her fiercely. "I love you. That's never going to change."

"And I love you. For always."